Secondhand Wishes

Secondhand Wishes

Anna Staniszewski

SCHOLASTIC PRESS
NEW YORK

All rights reserved. Published by Scholastic Press, an imprint of Scholastic Inc., *Publishers since 1920.*
SCHOLASTIC, SCHOLASTIC PRESS, and associated logos are trademarks and/or registered trademarks of
Scholastic Inc.

Library of Congress Cataloging-in-Publication Data available

ISBN 978-1-338-28017-3

10 9 8 7 6 5 4 3 2 1   19 20 21 22

Printed in the USA   23

First edition, February 2019

The text type was set in Adobe Caslon Pro

Book design by Yaffa Jaskoll

For the Cole family

Secondhand Wishes

Chapter 1

The day I found the wishing stones, I was running late. Really late. Like "disrupt the entire order of the universe" late.

Austin had thrown a fit at breakfast because he didn't want to drink the kale smoothie I made him. He said it looked like slime. (And okay, maybe it did.) After he dumped it all over himself in protest, I had to mop up the floor while Mom changed Austin's clothes.

When I finally got to the footbridge where Cassa and I always met in the morning, I was out of breath and she was gone. I glanced at my watch. Almost seven minutes behind schedule. Since I was never *ever* late, Cassa probably figured I wasn't coming. *Or maybe she walked to school with Marina instead and forgot all about you,* an annoying little voice inside me whispered.

I lingered there for a minute, drumming my fingers on my jeans, trying to decide if I should wait a little longer, just to be safe. But my watch was practically screaming at me to get moving, so I finally took off at a run, as if I could make up the time. But time doesn't care how fast you go when you're behind it. So the bell was already echoing through Adams Middle School as I rushed up the front steps. I sped through the seventh-grade hallway—without actually running because that was Not Allowed—and practically fell into first period.

"Late," Mrs. Connor said, pointing at me. Her finger felt like an arrow. "Detention."

"B-but—" I stammered, my stomach sinking into my knees.

"Sorry, Lexi." She tore a pink detention slip from the pad and dropped it on my desk. "Those are the rules."

Mrs. Connor was everyone's favorite math teacher, but she was also big on "tough love." I never thought she'd use it on me, though. I was plenty tough on myself already.

I tried to pay attention through the rest of class, making my notes on ratios and percentages perfectly color-coded for Friday's test. But my eyes kept wandering back to that pink piece of paper. How could I stay after school when I always helped out at the Antique Barn on Tuesdays?

After class, I hurried up to Mrs. Connor's desk, but she wouldn't even let me plead my case. "I know you're usually very punctual, Lexi, but the school has clear rules about tardiness."

"It's just that my brother . . ." I stopped, realizing that, unlike my previous teachers, Mrs. Connor had no idea about the genetic disorder that messed up Austin's intestines and made my family's life unpredictable. It would be nice to keep it that way, especially since Austin had been doing so much better lately. And really, it wasn't his fault I'd been late.

"I help out at an antique store after school on Tuesdays," I said instead, even though I knew that Cassa's mom would understand. "I really can't miss it." Being late to school *and* to work in one day was more bad karma than I could handle.

"You're a bit young for a job, aren't you?" Mrs. Connor asked, but she sounded impressed.

"I like doing it," I told her. And it meant I didn't have to ask my parents for an allowance. They had enough to worry about with all of Austin's medical bills.

"I'll tell you what," Mrs. Connor said. "How about you come to lunchtime detention, instead? It's all full today, but there should be room for one more student tomorrow."

"During lunch?" A tight feeling spread through my chest. Cassa and I had been sitting together at lunch every day for four years. I couldn't change my routine just like that! But I could tell by the look on Mrs. Connor's face that she wasn't going to budge, so I had no choice but to agree.

Normally, I was glad school had so many rules. It meant you always knew what you were supposed to be doing and when. Just this once, though, I wished she could have let things slide.

"Oh, and, Lexi," Mrs. Connor said as I turned to go. "I saw you got a B-plus on the last quiz. Nice improvement!"

I could only blink in response. Because even though my math grades had been getting better on the weekly quizzes, a B-plus was still far from good, at least for me. That's why I had to ace our first test.

When I got to lunch later that day, I sat down with Cassa at our usual corner table. I expected her to ask me where I'd been that morning, but she had her nose buried in a book about English castles. Her shoulders were hunched as if she were cold, but that usually meant she was really into whatever she was reading.

"Sorry I wasn't at the bridge earlier," I said, unzipping my lunch bag. "Things were kind of hectic this morning."

"What?" Cassa asked, glancing up from one of the glossy pages. "Oh, I thought I told you. Mom had to pick up some stuff for the store, so she dropped me off at school on her way."

Phew. She hadn't ditched me for Marina. Of course not. I was just being paranoid.

Cassa frowned across the table. "Is that an old sponge in your lunch?"

"Yup!" I said. "I saw this video the other day that said to use a frozen sponge instead of an ice pack to keep your food cold."

Cassa picked it up between two fingers. "Why?" she asked, wrinkling her nose.

"It costs less and doesn't weigh as much," I said. Then I noticed a moldy smell coming from the sponge. I groaned. "But I forgot to put it in plastic!" My wrapped sandwich was still edible, but a sniff of my apple told me it was a goner. Great. I'd have to scrub my lunch bag when I got home so Mom wouldn't throw it in the trash. She was a little nutty about protecting Austin from germs.

"Lexi's Life Hacks strike again!" Cassa said with a smile.

I self-consciously touched the industrial-strength hair clips on top of my head. Maybe trimming my own bangs using Scotch Tape hadn't been the best idea, but they were almost back to their normal length.

"So what happened this morning?" Cassa asked, offering me some of her baby carrots.

As I munched, I told her about the slime smoothie. "It's been taking Austin forever to get over a stomach bug, so when I saw a video about Leafy Green Diets, I thought it might help. But of course Austin wouldn't even take a sip." I sighed. "Mom was going on about how there was 'no convincing medical evidence' that the smoothie would do anything."

Cassa chuckled. "Plus, what four-year-old kid likes *kale?*"

I had to laugh too. "I guess it was kind of a stretch. Not even 'medical miracles' like to eat leaves."

That was what Mom was always calling Austin, her little medical miracle. Mom and Dad had always told me that one day I'd be an older sister, but it took years of doctors and tests and more doctors before it actually happened. Then Austin was born and we knew right away that something was wrong. It was as if the universe had finally given him to us, but with strings attached. No matter what we did, we couldn't seem to untie them.

My smile faded. "By the way, I got a detention for being late, so I won't be at lunch tomorrow, okay?"

"Wow," Cassa said, brushing her dark curls over her shoulder. "Lexi Block gets in trouble? I guess there's a first time for everything. Are you okay?"

"Fine," I said automatically. But I was all twitchy inside. Ever since school had started, I'd felt behind on my luck. I needed to catch up, and fast. "Maybe if I do really well on the math test, it'll balance stuff out."

"Of course you will," Cassa said. "You love math."

"I *did*," I corrected, "before Mrs. Connor changed how we do everything this year." I bit into my sandwich. "Anyway, if I get an A on this test, I know everything will be okay again."

I could tell Cassa didn't know what to say, but she didn't tell me to stop being ridiculous about my "balance of the universe" theory like other people would. That was one of the many reasons we'd been Sort-of Sisters since third grade. That was the year Austin was born with all his medical problems and Cassa's parents got divorced, and the two of us stuck together while our families were practically falling apart.

"Oh, hey! Check this out!" Cassa suddenly cried, pulling a neon green flyer out of her bag. "Look what I saw this morning."

"Dance club tryouts next week?" For a second, I could see it: me up onstage, spinning and twirling and losing myself in the music. Then I pictured myself messing up the steps, stumbling over someone's foot, and taking a bunch of other dancers down with me.

I quickly pushed the image out of my head. "Are you auditioning?"

"No way!" Cassa cried. "You know I trip over thin air. But you have to try out, Lexi. Remember when we used to make up dances and put on costumes and stuff? You were so good!"

"We were also eight." It was one thing to prance around in a tutu at your best friend's house where no one besides her cat could see you. It was another to get up onstage—without your best friend at your side, no less—and do a choreographed routine in front of the entire school. "Besides, I have my schedule for the year planned out already."

"Come on, Lex. Don't you ever get sick of doing the same thing all the time?" She chomped into a carrot. "Look at Marina. She's visited more countries than I've visited states! Did you know she's climbed the Eiffel Tower? Like, the real one? And she's been scuba diving and Jet Skiing and even spelunking!"

I nodded slowly, trying to act as if I knew what spelunking was. After Marina had moved into Cassa's neighborhood over the summer, her name had started popping up in all our conversations. She was nice enough, but the way I saw it, best friends were like shoes: There were only supposed to be two of you. Marina was like a third sneaker jammed onto someone's elbow. It was a good thing she had a different lunch period than we did, so at least I had Cassa to myself for part of the day.

"Marina only gets to travel so much because her mom's in the air force," I pointed out.

Cassa shook her head, as if I were missing the point. "I think we should try new stuff this year, that's all. Have new experiences. I'm thinking of checking out the knitting club."

"The knitting club? Aren't you allergic to wool?"

"I can make stuff out of cotton." She raised her eyebrows at me. "Promise you'll at least think about auditioning for the dance club?"

"Yeah, okay," I said, figuring it was easier to agree. I riffled in my bag and pulled out the hand sanitizer Mom insisted I use before *and* after meals. "Want some?" I asked.

But Cassa was hunched over her book again and didn't seem to hear me. I thought about using the rest of lunch to go over my math notes, but that wasn't right. Since when did Cassa and I sit together in silence as if we'd run out of things to say?

"Um, read anything interesting in there?" I finally asked.

Cassa's face lit up. "Yeah, actually! Did you know that spiral staircases in castles always go clockwise? That way if the enemy is going up the stairs with swords, they'll have a hard time fighting with their right hands."

"What happens if the enemy soldiers are left-handed?"

Cassa chuckled. "I guess they're the lucky ones!"

Soon, we were laughing and joking as usual, the odd silence between us gone. Phew. When the bell rang for the end of lunch, Cassa made a big show of putting the dance club flyer in my bag. I rolled my eyes dramatically and went off to social studies. Cassa's class had been assigned a time capsule project. But in mine, we had endless worksheets to go through every day, which I actually thought was more fun.

A few minutes later, I was straining to remember the capital of New Hampshire, when I heard my name over the loudspeaker. "Alexandra Block," the voice said, "please report to the main office." Uh-oh. The sandwich in my stomach was suddenly a clump of Play-Doh as I slung my bag over my shoulder and shuffled out of the room. Had Mrs. Connor told the principal about my detention?

When I got to the main office, everyone was bustling around or talking on the phone. I waited for someone to notice me. Finally, one of the secretaries nearly tripped over my foot on her way to the water cooler.

"Are you Alexandra?" the secretary asked. When I nodded, her face softened. "Your mom's on the phone. It's about your brother. He's in the hospital."

Chapter 2

"How bad is he?" I whispered to Mom on the other end of the phone. I was in an empty cubicle next to the vice principal's office, in an old desk chair that creaked like a rusty gate. Everyone in the main office was still bustling around me, but I could tell they were listening to every word I said.

Mom sighed. "Austin wouldn't eat lunch, and when he started to complain that his belly hurt, the school called me. The doctors said his stomach is pretty distended, so they're admitting him to do some scans and try to locate the intestinal blockage."

"He seemed fine this morning," I said, but that's how it always was. Austin would come down with a stomach bug or the flu or something, and we'd start to think that this time he'd actually get over it on his own. Then his digestive system would go haywire and he'd be back in the ER again.

"I know," Mom said with another sigh. "But the doctor said we caught it early this time. With any luck, he'll be home in the morning."

With any luck. My insides squeezed together as I remembered my detention. I'd already been pushing my luck with my bad math grades. Had being late that morning finally knocked everything out of balance?

"Dad cut his business trip short, but his flight doesn't get in until noon tomorrow," Mom went on. "So we'll need to make a plan for tonight."

"I still have some overnight stuff at Cassa's house from last time." I always stayed at Cassa's when Austin was in the hospital. It was the only good thing about the whole situation.

15

"Actually, no," Mom said. "I called Cassa's mom first, but she said they're redoing their kitchen and the house is pretty chaotic right now."

"Really?" That was the first I'd heard of it.

"So when Ms. Hinkley said they couldn't take you this time," Mom went on, her voice a little hesitant, "I had to come up with a backup plan."

My throat tightened. "What plan?"

"I asked your aunt if you could sleep over at her house tonight."

"Aunt Glinda?" I cried. "I can't stay with her! Last time she came over, she started crying during a cereal commercial, remember?" My mom's sister might have been named after the Good Witch of the North from *The Wizard of Oz*, but she was more like the Emotional Train Wreck Witch of the East.

"I know your aunt can be a bit . . . sensitive at times," Mom said, clearly choosing her words carefully. It was no secret that she and Aunt Glinda had always been polar opposites. "But she's in that big house all by herself. I think she could use the company." Mom sighed. "And we're out of options, Lexi. I need you to be flexible for me, okay?"

"Fine," I said, because she was right. Austin was sick. That's what mattered. It would be all right to stay with my aunt for one night. Tomorrow, things would go back to normal.

"Good," Mom said. "I'll tell Glinda you'll be at her house after you finish working at the Antique Barn."

"You mean I can't come to the hospital?" Cheering up my brother when he wasn't feeling well had always been my specialty.

Mom sighed for about the tenth time. "I'm afraid not, honey. Austin will be in and out of tests all afternoon. You'll see him tomorrow, okay?" I heard a muffled voice in the background. "Hold on. He wants to talk to you."

A second later, my brother whispered, "Lexi, can you do me a favor?"

He sounded a little out of it, but if he was asking for favors, things weren't so bad. "What do you need, buddy? Want me to feed your Ninja Turtles?" Or really, pretend to feed them, since they were plastic.

"Yeah, they get two pizzas each. Oh, and can you read with Batman?" he asked. Austin was still learning his letters, but he and Batman would spend hours looking at comics together. All superhero-themed, of course.

"Sure, buddy. I'll take care of it. And I'll see you when you get home tomorrow. Feel better, okay?"

"Okay." His voice was suddenly small.

"Make sure to tickle your feet for me," I told him. "And give your nose a honk."

That made Austin giggle. "Honk!" he said. Then he added, "LoveyouLexi," as if it were all one word, and hung up the phone.

* * *

After school, I hurried over to Felix Woods's locker. Fortunately, he was already there packing up his bag.

"How many do you need this time?" he asked when he saw me.

"Two," I said. "Actually, no. Make that three." I'd have almost no spending money left, but it would be worth it.

"You're in luck. I found a batch of new ones yesterday." He glanced around the hall to make sure there were no teachers nearby. Then he reached into his locker and took out a handful of perfect four-leaf clovers. After he placed three of them in my palm, I handed over my cash.

Felix looked around again and then pocketed the money. It was funny to see him acting like a shady criminal. With his innocent eyes and floppy dark hair, he could have passed for a cartoon puppy.

I couldn't imagine what he did with all his earnings. Everyone in school knew about Felix's side business, and his supply would always get dangerously low before big games and tests and dances.

"Thanks," I said as I carefully slipped the clovers into the small coin purse that I always kept with me. I wasn't sure I believed in all that four-leaf clover superstition, but it was better to be on the safe side. Even if it did mean forking over most of the money I earned at the antique shop.

"Thank *you*," Felix said, shutting his locker. "You're, like, my best customer."

"You must be the luckiest person on the planet to find so many clovers," I said.

Felix shrugged. "My mom's half Irish. That must be it."

"Huh, I thought your mom's family was from Vietnam," I said, remembering an ancestry report we'd all had to do back in fourth grade.

"They are, but some of them live in Ireland." Felix slung his bag over his shoulder. "Well, see ya!" he said before heading off to catch the bus.

When I went to meet Cassa in front of the school at our usual bench, she jumped to her feet. "Lexi! I heard them call your name over the loudspeaker. Is it Austin again?"

"Another stomach bug gone wrong," I said. "My mom called your mom about having me stay over, but she said you guys are redoing your kitchen?"

"I thought I told you." Cassa's forehead wrinkled. "Or maybe I told Marina. Anyway, Mom's finally replacing that gross linoleum and it's such a mess! We've been living on takeout for the past couple of days."

"Bummer," I said. "I guess that means I have to go stay with my weird aunt instead."

I waited for Cassa to insist that I stay at her house—that's what I would have done in a second if the situation were reversed. But instead she said, "That stinks!" And that was it.

We stood in silence for a minute because, really, what else was there to say? It would be weird to beg her to let me sleep over if she didn't want me to, right? Finally, I glanced at my watch. "We should go or we'll be late."

"Late for what?" Marina asked, appearing in front of us. She was wearing one of her brightly colored

necklaces that she'd beaded herself. It was pretty, I supposed, if you liked drawing attention to yourself. Then
again, Marina was one of the tallest girls in our grade,
so maybe she couldn't hide even if she wanted to.

"There you are," Cassa said. She turned to me.
"Marina's coming to check out the shop today. She's
going to love it, don't you think, Lex?"

I tried to smile, but my lips didn't want to cooperate.
Marina was coming to the shop now too? Maybe it was
silly, but the Antique Barn had always been mine and
Cassa's after-school thing. We'd never invited anyone to
come with us before.

As we left the school grounds, passing the old ceme-
tery next door, Cassa explained about her mom's store to
Marina. "She opened it right after she and my dad got
divorced, so she calls it her second husband." She laughed.
"The place is awesome, though. You never know what
you'll find. One time, I was looking for a book on Scottish
lochs, but none of the libraries had it and then—
poof!—it showed up at the shop! The exact book I

needed for my project! And another time, a lady was looking through the jewelry display, and she picked up this old ruby necklace she said was just like one her mom used to have. When she looked at the back, she realized it had her mom's initials engraved on it. Isn't that insane?"

"How did the necklace get there?" Marina asked. She was walking so fast on her long legs that I was practically running to keep up. Cassa didn't seem to notice that we were almost sprinting.

"I don't know," Cassa admitted. "The point is, there's like this magic to old things. Sometimes they pop up right when you need them. And every old lamp and book and teapot is on its own little adventure, you know?" Her voice took on the same dreamy quality it always did when she talked about the Antique Barn. I didn't know why she was so eager to try out knitting when it was obvious that she was happiest working at her mom's store.

Marina didn't look all that impressed. "So the shop is on Main Street? Is it anywhere near that bead store I was telling you about?"

"Beady Buy?" Cassa said. "Yeah, it's a block away."

"Can we go? I want to get some stuff for a new bracelet I'm working on."

"We don't have time," I jumped in, glancing at my watch. "We have to be at the Antique Barn at three thirty."

Marina let out a little "tsk" sound. "So we're a couple of minutes late. Who cares?"

We stopped at an intersection in front of the synagogue where Cassa and her mom went sometimes. As we waited to cross the street, I flashed Cassa a pleading look. "We really have to stick to the schedule," I said. Surely she'd understand why this was so important today.

"Why?" Marina asked. "You won't get *fired*, will you?" She giggled.

Cassa smiled back at her. "No. It's just that Lexi has a deal with the universe."

I glanced at the ground, my face suddenly hot. My theory wasn't exactly a secret, but whenever I'd tried to tell anyone else about it, they never understood. Why would Cassa bring it up?

Sure enough, Marina frowned and asked, "What does that mean?"

The light changed and the "Walk" sign turned on, but Marina was clearly not going to move until I explained. "Think of the universe as one of those two-sided scales," I said. "If something bad happens on one side, you have to put something good on the other side to balance it out."

Her frown grew deeper. "Why would the universe care about you being on time?"

"Because it's a good thing."

"You know when it's supposed to snow," Cassa jumped in, "and you do all your homework because you know if you don't, then there's definitely going to be school the next day? Well, it's like that. You do the homework so you get a snow day."

"You do everything right so that nothing goes wrong," I added.

Marina shrugged as the "Do Not Walk" sign started flashing. "Okay, I get it," she said. But I could tell she didn't. Even so, that didn't mean I could give up on trying to keep the universe happy, not when there was so much to lose.

"Come on," I said. "We should go."

But Cassa didn't move. "Lex?" she said, winding one of her curls around her finger. "I do kind of want to check out the bead store. You don't mind going ahead on your own, do you? And we'll meet you at the Barn in a few?"

I stared at her for a second, sure she was joking. Maybe she didn't totally buy into the whole idea of keeping the universe happy, but she knew how important it was to me. How could she change our routine just like that, especially when Austin needed my help? I mean, she didn't even *like* beads. But Cassa didn't look like she was kidding. Instead, there was something like a pleading look on her face.

"N-no," I said finally. "I don't mind, I guess. If that's what you want to do."

"You're the best!" Cassa said, her face exploding into a bright smile. Then she grabbed Marina's arm and the two of them hurried away, leaving me standing at the corner by myself.

Chapter 3

When I got to the Antique Barn, I scanned the rows of weathered tables, dressers overflowing with knick-knacks, and old clocks hanging from beams in the ceiling. It was perfectly controlled chaos, which was part of what I liked about helping out here, that and the comforting smell of pine that always hung in the air. I took a deep breath and waited for the dusty, familiar feeling of being in the shop to settle over me. But being there didn't feel right without Cassa.

"Where's my daughter hiding?" Ms. Hinkley called from behind the counter. It had been made from a couple of old wagon wheels, a "great find" at one of the antique shows that Cassa and her mom were always visiting.

"Cassa's on her way over," I said, not wanting to go into details.

"How's your brother?" Ms. Hinkley's face was full of concern. "I'm sorry we can't have you stay with us this time, but you'll be okay with your aunt, won't you?"

"Austin will be fine. I'll be fine. We'll *all* be fine," I practically squawked. Desperate to change the subject, I added, "Cassa told me you picked up some things this morning?"

Ms. Hinkley nodded and led me to a pile of boxes in the back of the store. "A couple of nice armoires, and a box of odds and ends. Oh, and when I got to the shop, I found a few cartons on the steps. Would you mind sorting through everything?"

"Sure." That happened a lot, people dumping their old stuff in front of the store. Maybe it was easier to have someone else throw some of your memories away for you.

"As always, if there's anything you like, feel free to put it aside for yourself," Ms. Hinkley said.

"Thanks." That was technically one of the perks of helping out at the Barn. Cassa was always bringing stuff home from the store, but I'd never found anything that spoke to me.

"I'll be in the back office. Give a shout if anyone comes in, okay?" Ms. Hinkley asked.

I nodded and pulled on some plastic gloves. When I opened one of the boxes, my eyes stung from the dust. It was clear no one had looked at this stuff in years, and I could see why. The box was full of broken toys and yellowed books and musty T-shirts with weird band names, nothing you'd bother to remember.

As I sorted through the items, my muscles slowly relaxed. No matter how out of control life felt, putting things in order always made me calmer. After a few minutes, I had four separate piles on the floor: Trash,

Recycle, Keep, and Maybe. The Maybe pile was the one I kept agonizing over, so I was glad Ms. Hinkley would make the final decision.

Satisfied, I opened the next box. On top was a shoebox full of ticket stubs from concerts and a stack of tattered teen magazines. I put them all into the Recycle pile and kept digging. Underneath an unused calendar from over twenty years ago and a couple of creepily smiling dolls with neon hair, I found a small velvet bag. The fabric used to be soft and black, but now it was faded and matted. It felt as though there were marbles inside, but the shape of them was wrong. They clinked together as I pulled open the bag. Inside, I found four shiny stones, about the size of chocolate coins, each a different shade of gray. Each had a word written on it: *Friendship, Family, Health,* and *Success.*

What were these?

I glanced at the velvet bag again and read the small tag hanging from the string. *Magical Wishing Stones,* it said in loopy cursive. Then, in smaller letters: *Make a wish and let the magic of the stones bring luck and happiness to all areas of your life.*

Um, okay. What kind of magical kit had *four* of something? There were always three wishes in fairy tales, and it was always the seventh son of the seventh son who did big important things in fantasy novels. Even *five* stones would have been better than four! Then again, four-leaf clovers were supposed to bring good luck, so maybe it wasn't that weird.

I poured the stones back into the bag and cinched up the top, but I couldn't quite make myself put them in the Trash pile. I knew avoiding sidewalk cracks to ward off bad luck was silly—not to mention handing all my money over to Felix—but I did it on the off chance that it might keep the universe happy. I didn't believe in magic, definitely not the way Cassa did, but maybe there was a chance these stones had some good energy attached to them too.

Just then, the front door jingled open, and Cassa's deep laugh echoed through the store.

"Those earrings are going to look so good on you when they're done!" Marina was saying. I could just see the top of her head over one of the shelves, but she couldn't see me.

"We can make them on Friday, after we work on our time capsule project," Cassa said. "I know! We could have a sleepover at my house."

"Sure!" Marina said. "That would be fun."

I couldn't believe it. Cassa didn't want me to sleep over when I desperately needed a place to stay, but she hadn't thought twice about inviting Marina? And it wasn't only that. It was Cassa always going on about how great Marina was, and telling her about things first, and wanting to spend every spare minute with her. Ever since school had started, it was as though my best friend had started to forget about me. And the more she saw Marina, the worse things got.

I squeezed the bag of wishing stones in my hand so tightly that my palm hurt. Then, on a whim, I pulled out the Friendship stone again, curled my fingers around it, and closed my eyes. "I wish Cassa and Marina wouldn't talk to or see each other anymore," I whispered.

I waited for a second, hoping to feel a tingle or a zap, some sign that my wish had worked. Of course, there was nothing. Nothing but Marina and Cassa's laughter still echoing through the shop.

With an angry sigh, I grabbed the bag of stones and threw the Friendship one inside. I pulled the bag shut and tossed it on top of the Trash pile. Finally, I yanked off my gloves and dropped them next to the two unopened boxes.

Then I marched out of the Barn, straight past Cassa and Marina.

"Hey, Lex. Where are you going?" Cassa called.

But I didn't dare stop. Instead, I took off at a run, focusing on stepping exactly in the center of the sidewalk and breathing in time with my strides—step and step, and breath and breath, and step and step, and breath and breath—until there wasn't room in my brain for anything else.

Chapter 4

When I got to Aunt Glinda's house, I leaned against the front gate for a minute, trying to catch my breath. Back when Grandma Jean had lived here, I vaguely remembered the house looking cheerful and bright, but now that it was only Aunt Glinda, the paint had started to chip and the house generally looked tired. I knew how it felt.

It was strange to be at the house by myself. Usually my family only went over to Aunt Glinda's on her birthday. We didn't see much of her besides that, other than holidays at our place. Mom said it was because her sister was "a bit of a loner," but I wondered how someone could spend so much time by herself in such a cluttered old house. It would drive me insane.

"Lexi?" a voice said behind me.

I turned to find Elijah Lewis-Green standing by the driveway. I hadn't seen him since he'd started being homeschooled last spring, but he still wore jeans covered in hand-drawn cartoons and blue glasses that popped against his dark skin. He could have been a character from one of his favorite comics.

"Hey, Elijah," I said. "Um, what's up?"

"I have something for you," he said, pulling a rolled-up piece of paper out of his pocket. "I heard your brother was sick again. I made this for him."

I was about to ask Elijah how he'd heard about Austin, but then I remembered that one of his moms was a nurse at the hospital. I unrolled the paper—a drawing of Austin dressed up as Batman—and smiled. "Wow, thanks. How did you know he's into Batman?"

"I remember you talking about his Halloween costume last year." Elijah shrugged. "Well, see ya." Then he flashed a small smile, hopped on his skateboard, and rode away.

Only after Elijah had disappeared around the corner did I think to wonder how he'd known I was going to be at Aunt Glinda's house. Then I noticed my aunt waving to me from the front window. I carefully slipped the drawing into my bag in between my color-coded notebooks and then ventured up the sagging porch stairs.

Inside, the house reeked of mustiness and burned molasses.

"Lexi!" Aunt Glinda singsonged from the kitchen. "Guess what just came out of the oven!"

I dabbed at my sweaty forehead with my sleeve and then reluctantly peeked into the kitchen, trying not to cough. My aunt was decked out in one of Grandma Jean's flowery aprons, holding a heaping plate of what looked like tiny brown bricks. That explained the terrible molasses smell.

"How was school?" Aunt Glinda asked in a fake chipper voice, as if we were acting out a scene from a

TV show. "How many cookies would you like? Two? Three?"

My throat threatened to close up. It was clear Aunt Glinda was trying to make me feel at home. I didn't want to hurt her feelings, but I also didn't want to risk breaking my teeth.

"Thanks. I don't want to spoil my dinner," I finally said. Too late, I noticed a pot of something greenish bubbling on the stove.

"Oh, that's my spinach stew," Aunt Glinda said, following my gaze. "I found a recipe for it in one of your grandmother's cookbooks. I didn't have all the ingredients, but I think it should still be good."

I glanced around my aunt's mess of a kitchen, which was in serious need of some life hacks. She didn't even have her spices stored in mason jars! No wonder she couldn't keep track of which ingredients she needed.

Aunt Glinda finally gave up and put the cookies down on the table. "I'm so glad we get to spend a little time together," she said. "When your mom called me,

I jumped at the chance to help. I only wish poor Austin was feeling better."

"Do you know how he's doing?"

Aunt Glinda's smiled faded. "He's okay, but they're thinking about keeping him longer than one night to be safe." She put a hand on my shoulder. "The good news is that you can go see him tonight after all. We can stop by your house on the way to the hospital to pick up some clothes for you."

I was glad about the last part at least, but my heart still sagged. So much for catching Austin's stomach problems early this time. But he'd be fine. He had to be.

"Thanks," I told my aunt. I pulled Elijah's drawing out of my bag. "I'll have to make sure to bring this for him. My, um, friend made it."

Aunt Glinda's face lit up. "How nice! Was this your friend Cassandra?"

"Cassa," I corrected. "And no, it wasn't her. She's . . ." But what could I say? She's not my friend anymore? She's been brainwashed by an alien named Marina

39

who's probably taking her back to the mother ship right now? "I think it'll cheer Austin up," I said instead.

"It certainly will," Aunt Glinda said. "What's this?" She held up a piece of neon paper that had stuck to the edge of the drawing.

"Oh, nothing." I tried to grab the flyer back, but it was too late.

"*Dance club tryouts. Round 1 on Monday after school in the gym?*" Aunt Glinda read. "Are you going to audition?" Her voice was suddenly full of excitement. "I remember when we used to put on music when you were a baby, and you'd jiggle your little behind. It was adorable!"

I cringed, remembering a video Mom had taken at the Fourth of July parade when I was a toddler. I'd gotten so into dancing that I toppled over and face-planted on the grass, accidentally taking another kid down with me. How embarrassing. That had been the last time I'd performed in public.

"I don't know how that flyer got in my bag," I said. "There's no way I could do the club, anyway. Even if I got in, rehearsals run late, and I'm not allowed to walk home after dark."

"That's easy. I'd pick you up!" Aunt Glinda said.

"Don't you have to work?" My aunt had been a receptionist at the same nursing home ever since she'd graduated from high school. She liked to say that the "old folks" there depended on her, but I'd once heard my mom say that Aunt Glinda needed them as much as they needed her. Since I was pretty sure my aunt never left the house to go anywhere other than work, maybe that was true.

Aunt Glinda waved her hand dismissively. "I'll figure it out." She smiled. "See? Now you have no excuse."

"But—"

"No excuse!" Aunt Glinda repeated. "Trust me, Lexi. You can't let excuses hold you back in life. I've certainly learned that the hard way."

"I don't want to be in the dance club," I insisted. But as the words came out of my mouth, I knew they weren't true. I *did* want to.

I hadn't admitted this to anyone, not even Cassa, but last year I'd come really close to auditioning. I'd run through the dance routine so many times, I could have performed it backward. Jumping around my room to the pounding music had made me feel so free, so totally out of control—in a good way. But when the day of the audition came, the thought of being with all those people I didn't really know, of totally changing my schedule, of doing something without Cassa, and of making a complete fool out of myself, had been too much. That's why I'd chickened out.

But now Cassa's doing stuff without you, that annoying little voice inside me whispered.

"There!" Aunt Glinda said from the other end of the kitchen. She'd written *Lexi's dance audition* in big letters on the calendar on the fridge. "Now you have to do it. And I'll pick you up afterward so we can celebrate, okay?" She laughed. "Sometimes the best way to get yourself to do something is to write it down. I've been dragging my feet on cleaning out this house, but I made a list and now I'm finally tackling it."

Wow. I'd never really thought of my aunt as a doer, but she was clearly on a mission. I must have looked surprised because Aunt Glinda added, "You start to see life differently once you turn a certain age, I guess. You realize you need to start moving forward instead of looking backward."

"Have you been talking to my mom?" I asked. That was one of her favorite sayings.

Aunt Glinda shrugged. "I think she has been rubbing off on me. Anyway, I found an old hamster cage when I was cleaning out my closet this morning. Can you believe it? I haven't had a hamster since I was about your age!" Suddenly, her eyes got a little misty. "Captain Squeak was such a sweet little guy."

I took a step back. Would it be rude to make an excuse and run away before my aunt started crying?

Luckily the kitchen phone rang at that moment. Aunt Glinda quickly wiped her eyes and answered it in an overly cheerful voice. "Oh, sure!" she said after a second. "She's right here!" Then she handed me the receiver. "It's Cassandra."

"Tell her I'm not here," I whispered. For once I was glad that my parents insisted we couldn't afford to get me a cell phone.

Aunt Glinda shook her head. "She sounds upset."

Huh. Maybe Cassa felt bad about what had happened that afternoon. I finally took the phone. "Hello?"

"Lexi, I'm so glad you're there," Cassa said in a rush. "I don't know what to do. It's Marina. I can't find her anywhere."

"Wh-where did she go?"

"I don't know. That's what I'm trying to tell you!" Cassa cried. "She disappeared!"

"Disappeared?" I repeated. "What do you mean?"

Cassa let out a sigh of frustration. "After you ran out of the Barn, Marina was saying something to me and

44

then—poof!—she just vanished. I know it sounds insane, and my mom won't believe me! She keeps saying, 'I don't know what game you girls are playing, but I have work to do.' I'm telling you, Lex, she's gone!"

"Wow, okay."

"Can you call her for me? Her phone rings but then it sounds like someone picks up and then nothing, just silence."

"Oh, I don't know . . ." I'd never talked to Marina on the phone before.

"Please, Lexi? I want to make sure she's okay. Maybe I should call the police or something!"

"Whoa, the police?" Cassa wasn't usually the kind of person to overreact to things. If she was this worried, then I had to help. "Okay, I'll call her. I'm sure she's fine." I wrote down the number Cassa gave me and then gave it a call.

"Hello?" Marina said after only one ring.

"Hey, um, it's Lexi. Cassa wanted me to call you to, um, make sure that—"

"Is this some kind of joke?" she broke in. "Is it like a prank you pull on the new kids or something?"

"Huh?"

"Look, if you didn't want me hanging out with you guys, just say so. You didn't have to have Cassa do a whole disappearing act on me."

"Disappearing act?"

"Come on. You were in on it too, weren't you? One minute I'm standing there with Cassa, and the next minute, she's gone. Was it like a smoke-and-mirrors thing? And then she keeps calling me and not saying anything? Why? To mess with me?"

This didn't make sense. Cassa saying that Marina had disappeared. Marina saying that Cassa had disappeared. Maybe *I* was the one they were playing a joke on!

"Well?" Marina demanded. When I didn't answer, she let out a frustrated groan and added, "Fine! Whatever!" Then she hung up.

What was going on? My brain felt as though it were coated in burned molasses as the pieces slowly started to fit together.

Because maybe this wasn't a joke. Maybe this was something else.

I'd wished for Cassa and Marina to stop seeing and talking to each other, hadn't I? Obviously this wasn't what I'd had in mind, but it had still happened. Which had to mean that my wish had worked. It had really worked!

A shiver went through me from head to toe. I couldn't believe it! Maybe some silly shiny stones *could* bring luck to your life after all.

Chapter 5

In the morning, I woke up in a panic. That always happened when I spent the night somewhere that wasn't home. My brain would race through all the unfamiliar stuff around me, and for a second, I'd feel as though I were falling through empty space. But then I recognized the flowery bedspread and the ugly seagull paintings on the walls, and I remembered that I was at Aunt Glinda's house, and I could breathe again.

As I sat up in the lumpy bed and yawned, my jaw cracked the way it did every morning. My teeth were aching from being clenched so tightly during the night. Even when I was asleep, I guess I was still worrying.

Right now, most of my worrying had to do with Austin. Luckily, my brother had been his usual goofy self when Aunt Glinda and I had visited him last night. He'd been busy making a tower out of a bunch of little paper cups that he'd convinced the nurses to give him. But he was also clearly in pain and grumpy about having to sleep in a hospital bed. It stabbed at me to think he might have to spend another night there. At least Elijah's drawing had made him smile.

Then—in a flash that practically made me jump out of bed—I remembered the other big thing that had happened yesterday. My Friendship wish had come true! Okay, maybe it was crazy to assume that the wishing stones had worked. But Cassa and Marina *had* had some sort of falling-out. That meant things between Cassa and me would be back to normal in no time.

My body was buzzing with excitement as I hurried to get ready for school. I even found myself humming a little as I pinned my bangs back and pulled my hair into its usual two braids. (Ponytails always gave me a headache, which Dad joked was because my head was screwed on too tight.) But when I went into the kitchen to grab breakfast, I found Aunt Glinda sitting at the table staring out the window. She was still in her pajamas and looked as though she'd been crying.

"Oh, Lexi," she said, dabbing at her nose with a tissue. "Good. You're up."

My excitement evaporated. "What's wrong? Is it Austin?"

"No, no. Nothing's wrong. I'm a bit overwhelmed this morning, that's all. I have the day off from work, and I was going to spend it cleaning the house. But the thought of going through more of my old things is starting to get to me." She tried to smile. "Do you want some oatmeal? I put prunes in it to sweeten it up."

"Um, sure," I said, afraid turning her down would make her weepy again. This was such a change from the way she'd been yesterday. What happened to all her "no excuses" talk?

"I'll go get dressed so I can drive you to school," Aunt Glinda said.

"That's okay. I can walk." If I left nine minutes earlier than my usual time, I'd get to first period without a problem. But my aunt told me to stop being silly and hurried off to get ready.

After I'd choked down as much breakfast as I could and brushed my teeth, my aunt still hadn't come out of her room. So I killed time by organizing the avalanche of plastic bags under her kitchen sink by putting them into an empty tissue box that I found in the recycling bin. It was one of the first "life hacks" I'd done at my house a couple of years ago, before I'd gotten hooked on them.

"Wow, what's all this?" Aunt Glinda asked when she came back into the kitchen. She seemed a lot more pulled together now.

I held up the box, which was stuffed full of plastic bags, before tucking it back under the sink. "That way you can keep them in one place."

"Genius!" Aunt Glinda said. "Maybe I should have you organize my entire house."

I could tell she was mostly kidding, but honestly that did sound kind of fun. The house could certainly use it. "Maybe next time I'm over, I can put your spices in order," I offered.

Aunt Glinda beamed. "Perfect!" She opened the fridge. "Want to take some of the leftover spinach stew for lunch today?"

"That's okay!" I said, a little too loudly. "I usually buy lunch." I felt bad lying, but I'd rather take my chances with cafeteria food. Besides, I hadn't had time to de-mold my lunch bag yet. There was probably some awesome life hack way of doing it.

Aunt Glinda looked disappointed that I'd rejected her stew, but she only waved me out to her car. As we sped out of her neighborhood, she turned on some loud music, the kind of classic rock stuff my dad listened to sometimes. I would have thought Aunt Glinda would be more into sad ballads about people watching it rain outside.

"With any luck, Austin will be home by this afternoon," she said when we pulled into the school driveway. "But if not, I'll pick you up right here after school and bring you to the hospital, okay?"

I smiled. After what had happened between Cassa and Marina, I was starting to think I'd finally stumbled onto some good luck. "Thanks, Aunt Glinda."

"No problem, kiddo," she said. Then she drove away.

Cassa was waiting for me at my locker. "I almost stopped at the bridge to wait for you, but then I remembered you were coming from your aunt's house." She was talking to me, but her eyes were darting all over the hallway.

"What's wrong?" I asked.

"Just seeing if Marina's here. I'm still worried about her."

"I told you, she's fine." I hadn't known how to explain about the two of them not being able to see each other. It sounded completely bananas. And even though I hoped that it meant my wish had come true, I couldn't be sure.

Cassa shrugged. "It's so crazy, you know? One minute things seem fine and the next minute they're not."

"Yeah," I said softly. That's how things had been feeling between me and Cassa for weeks now.

At that moment, I spotted Marina walking down the hall. I held my breath, waiting for Cassa to notice her. It was hard not to when she towered over most of the kids around us. But Cassa didn't. Even though she was looking right at Marina, her expression stayed blank.

I could tell the minute Marina saw me, though, because her entire face tensed. "Hey, Lexi," she said, walking right past Cassa without even glancing at her. "So where is she?"

"Huh?" I asked.

"Cassa? I figured you two would be standing around, waiting for me so you could laugh in my face."

"No," I said. "It's not like that."

"Not like what?" Cassa asked, giving me a strange look. "What are you talking about?"

"Um."

And then Cassa and Marina were both looking at me expectantly, and it dawned on me, *really* dawned on me, that there was something seriously bizarre going on. Because even though they were inches apart, the two of them couldn't hear each other. They couldn't even see each other!

I had no idea what to do. Luckily, the first bell rang, so I mumbled an excuse that was aimed at both of them and hurried away.

Okay, maybe this wishing business was more complicated than I'd realized. But Cassa and Marina weren't going to be spending every second together anymore, which meant that I would have my best friend back. That was the important thing.

* * *

I got to my first ever lunchtime detention with a tray of slightly gray lasagna clutched in my hands. I expected to see a room of brooding delinquents slumped in their seats, throwing spitballs or carving their initials into their desks. Instead, the kids were sitting in a circle, chatting and munching on their lunches as if this were a free period.

"Okay, let's quiet down," Mrs. Connor said. Huh. I guess she ran the detention. "Before we start today's discussion, I want us to go around and introduce ourselves since you might not all know one another."

Discussion? Was this detention, or had I stumbled into some sort of support group? The kids, a mix of sixth through eighth graders, took turns saying their names and why they were in detention. Most of them had been late or broken some minor rule, but a couple of girls had gotten into a shoving match during lunch.

I was afraid to make eye contact with them, in case they decided they wanted to push me around too.

"Now then," Mrs. Connor said. "Let's talk about what you can do to avoid being sent here in the future, all right?" She pointed at me. "Lexi? Do you want to go first?"

I had no idea what to say besides "I won't be late again."

"Let's dig deeper than that," Mrs. Connor said. "How might you avoid this pattern of behavior in the future?"

Pattern of behavior? Was she serious? I'd been late *one time*! Suddenly, I wished I'd told her all about Austin. Maybe then she would have let me out of this whole stupid detention thing.

"Come on, Lexi. This is a safe space where you can work on improving your habits."

"I don't have bad habits," I blurted out. "I'm always on time. All I do is try to make everything perfect!"

Mrs. Connor gave me a look of disappointment. "Remember that perfection is impossible," she said. "But improvement isn't."

I didn't know what that was supposed to mean. Thankfully, she'd moved on to her next victim. I slumped in my chair and sliced into my lasagna, but my appetite was gone.

Chapter 6

Right before the final bell rang, I heard my name on the loudspeaker again. "Alexandra Block," the secretary's voice said.

My stomach clenched. It was Austin. It had to be.

When I got to the office, I expected to have to talk to Mom on the phone again. Instead, Dad was standing there waiting for me. His thinning hair was sticking up funny and his shirt was so wrinkled, it reminded me of used tissue paper.

"Hey, Lex," he said, pulling me into a hug. It was good to see him, but he shouldn't be here yet.

"I thought Aunt Glinda was picking me up."

"I flew in early. And boy, are my arms tired!" He gave me a goofy, openmouthed grin.

"Dad!" I said with a groan. If he was making his usual lame jokes, maybe things weren't so bad. But clearly something was wrong. "No really, why are you here?"

His grin faded. "I don't want you to worry," he said slowly, as if putting off telling me the bad news. "Your brother is going to be fine. But they're taking him into surgery today."

"But he's not supposed to have another operation for months!"

"The doctors have decided this is the best strategy right now."

Emergency surgery. We'd gone through this before, when Austin was first born and a couple of times since. He'd stay in the hospital for days and days after an operation, recovering, and everyone would always say things would be okay, fine, great, but that never made me worry less. Now it was happening yet again. No matter what I did, no matter how much good I tried to put on one side of the cosmic scale, it never seemed to balance out the bad.

But this time, maybe there *was* something more I could do.

"Can we stop at the Antique Barn on the way to the hospital? There's something I need to pick up."

Dad looked surprised, but he didn't object. I guess he was used to my odd requests by now.

When I opened the car door, empty fast-food bags spilled out of the front seat. "Just toss them in the back," Dad said, looking a little sheepish.

As I added them to the pile of trash next to Austin's car seat, I couldn't help remembering how clean Dad's car used to be. Mom would make fun of him for taking better care of it than of our house. But that was before Austin was born and Dad had to take on extra business trips to help pay the hospital bills. He'd practically been living in cars and planes and hotel rooms ever since.

"You know, I could make a trash bin for your car out of a cereal container," I said.

"That's okay. I'll clean the car out one of these days." He chuckled. "Or sell it and let someone else deal with the mess."

"At least let me do an air freshener," I said. "I saw a cool video about how to make one out of a clothespin and some cotton balls." Yes, it was probably less work to just buy a car air freshener, but where was the fun in that?

"Lexi, don't worry about it. Really." Dad glanced over at me as we stopped at a red light. "How are you doing? Are you okay?"

"Fine," I said. Fine, fine, fine. How could I admit to being anything else when my parents were already so stressed out?

"This could be the last surgery," he said when we started moving again. "The doctors said that if Bug heals okay from this one, we might be in the clear."

Could. Might. When it came to Austin, we never used words that actually meant anything.

When we pulled up to the Antique Barn, I ran inside and found Ms. Hinkley sitting at the counter eating some yogurt.

"Lexi, is everything all right?" she asked, putting down her spoon. Her eyes flicked over to my dad waiting in the car.

"Yes, um . . ." I didn't know how to explain, so I forged ahead with something like the truth. "I left something here yesterday, and I wanted to get it because I thought it might be good luck."

Her face softened. "Sure. Grab whatever you need."

But when I got to the back of the store, I realized my piles were gone. "Ms. Hinkley!" I cried, running over to her. "The stuff I went through yesterday, where is it? The trash pile? Where's the trash pile?"

"Oh, I . . ." She blinked. "I put it in the bins out back. You were right, none of it was worth keeping."

I dashed to the back door and threw it open. Then I rushed over to the line of trash bins. Normally, I wouldn't even think about touching them without gloves on, but this was an emergency. I pulled off one lid after another, riffling through broken clothes hangers, greasy take-out containers, and packing peanuts.

And then, finally, under a moth-eaten curtain, I found the velvet bag. The tag was stained with what looked like coffee, but when I opened the bag, all four stones were inside.

I poured them into my hand, the stones clinking together in my palm. There it was. The Health stone. I squeezed it as tightly in my fingers as I could, closed my eyes, and wished.

Chapter 7

At the hospital, we waited and waited for Austin to get out of surgery. After some pacing, Dad settled in to answer work emails on his iPad and told me I should try to get some homework done. But there was no way I could focus. I was so jittery with nerves, my legs couldn't stay still and my fingers couldn't stop tapping on my notebook. The wishing stone had to work. It had to. Then we'd never have to worry about Austin being sick again.

"Feel like taking a walk?" Dad finally asked when my hands and feet were practically doing a drumroll.

"How about you go get us some snacks from the cafeteria?"

"But what if—"

"Take my phone," Dad said, slipping it into my hand along with some cash. "If we hear anything, I'll call you from the nurses' station."

I grabbed my bag and headed down the hall of the children's wing. It had been a while since we'd been here, but I still remembered my way around. It felt strange to be by myself, though. In the past, Mom or Dad was always with me. Now I was riding the elevator alone, surrounded by nurses in scrubs and old folks with walkers. As I got out on the ground floor, even though there were people bustling all around me, I suddenly felt totally alone.

Amazingly, the first person I saw when I walked into the cafeteria was Elijah Lewis-Green. At that second, he looked up and waved.

I bought some snacks for my dad and a lemonade for myself and then headed to Elijah's table. Even though I barely knew the guy, I was suddenly glad to see him.

"Hey," he said, pushing up his blue glasses. "Grab a seat."

"Thanks," I said, plopping down opposite him. There were drawings spread out across the entire table. "What are you doing here?"

"My mom's shift is up soon, so I'm waiting until she's done." He moved some of the papers aside so I could put my food down. "How are things going?"

I started to say "fine," but the truth slipped out instead. "My brother is in surgery right now. It's taking forever. You don't think that's a bad sign, do you?"

Elijah shook his head. "My mom—Mama Dee—is a nurse, and she always says that surgeries take as long as they take. Nothing we can do about it."

"But we *should* be able to do something about it," I said. "It's not fair that we have to sit and wait."

"Yeah, it's not fair," Elijah said matter-of-factly. He was so calm and relaxed about everything. I tried to imagine what that would feel like, but it seemed impossible.

"So what are you drawing?" I asked.

He glanced down at his scattered sketches. "You know how I made that Batman picture for your brother? I started thinking that I could make cards for the other sick kids here. I spend so much time at the hospital anyway, you know? Might as well use it to make something awesome."

"Wow, that's really nice of you," I said. "Thanks again, by the way. My brother loved the picture." I glanced at my dad's phone. No missed calls.

Elijah shrugged and started sketching again. "Yeah, no problem."

Silence fell between us, but it wasn't the loud kind of silence that had been happening with Cassa lately. Elijah drew and I sipped my lemonade, and it was actually nice to quietly coexist for a minute.

"What's it like being homeschooled?" I asked after a while.

"It's good," he said. "There are tests and lessons I have to do, but my moms let me set my own schedule so

I still have time for art. That way I don't get bored like I did with regular school."

I couldn't imagine being home all day with no real schedule. "But how do you know if you're spending time doing the right things?"

"I guess I don't worry about it." Elijah smirked as he glanced down at my hands. Without realizing it, I'd started putting his drawings into neat little piles. "You should try not worrying sometime. It's kind of nice."

I snorted. "I'm pretty sure I was born worrying. My mom says that I started grinding my teeth before I even *had* teeth."

That made Elijah laugh, and I couldn't help smiling too. For a second, at least, I felt a little lighter.

Then Dad's phone started buzzing in my hands. "Hello?" I said, my voice barely a whisper.

"Austin is out of surgery," Dad said on the other end.

I leaped to my feet. "Gotta go," I told Elijah. I barely heard his reply as I ran out of the cafeteria. Only when I was in the elevator did I realize that I'd forgotten the snacks I'd bought. But there was no way I was going to waste time going back to get them.

In the waiting room, Dad was standing at the window, staring out at the buildings below us.

"What's going on?" I nearly shouted. "How is he?"

Dad turned toward me, and I was stunned to see him smiling. Really smiling. "The surgery went perfectly," he said. "The doctor said this might be it, Lex. This might be the last time."

I let out a long, long breath, as if I'd been holding it for years. It had worked. My wish had worked! Maybe Elijah's positive attitude was rubbing off on me, because even though Dad had said the dreaded "might" word, I knew, just *knew*, that Austin was finally going to be okay.

Chapter 8

After Austin was back in his hospital room and "resting comfortably," Dad insisted that Mom and I head home for the night. "Go get some rest," he told us. "Bug and I will be fine here." Dad had looked exhausted earlier that day, but he was all smiles now.

When I got home, I used my mom's computer to check my email and found one from Cassa wondering how Austin was doing. *Are we still on for Saturday night??* she asked at the end. For once, she hadn't said anything about inviting Marina along, and it made me smile in relief. Things between us were fine. I didn't have to doubt that anymore.

I quickly wrote back to let her know Austin was okay and that our usual Saturday-night plans were on. I couldn't wait to eat popcorn and Junior Mints without Marina judging us for mixing them together, and to watch the latest episode of *Unbelievable Medical Mysteries*, the one about the boy who was born with his heart outside his body. Cassa would probably be grossed out as usual, but I loved those shows. If people could go through that kind of bizarre medical stuff and be okay at the end, then surely Austin would be fine.

When I got into my pajamas and climbed into bed, for once I didn't have the feeling that there was something I was forgetting, something I should be doing. And for the first time in a long time, I actually fell asleep without worrying.

When I woke up in the morning, something was off. But I was in my own bed. Everything in my room was where it was supposed to be. And Austin was okay.

When I sat up, I finally realized what was different. My jaw didn't hurt! I had to laugh as I remembered my conversation with Elijah. Maybe my lifetime habit of grinding my teeth was finally over.

Mom had all our bowls and plates out on the counter when I went into the kitchen.

"What's all this?" I asked.

"I figured I'd run them through the dishwasher again," she said. "Never can be too careful with the things we eat off of."

I knew what she really meant was that we could never be too careful with the things *Austin* ate off of. Even though those dishes were already sparkling clean and he probably wouldn't be home for days. But this was how we coped with things in my family. I obsessed and Mom sanitized. Austin had obviously gotten most of his personality from Dad. Lucky kid.

"Here," Mom said, handing me a cereal bowl that was still scalding hot from the dishwasher. "This one should be clean."

As I went to pour myself some Cheerios, Mom said, "After you're done eating, we can head over to the hospital."

"Wait, what? I have to go school." I wanted to visit my brother, of course, but what if messing up my schedule knocked things out of balance again?

"Lexi, you can miss one day. You have a good excuse."

"I know, but . . ." But there was no way to explain it in a way that my mom would understand.

"You are so much like your grandmother some-times," Mom said, giving me a warm smile. "She was pretty much married to her routine. I'm afraid that since Austin was born, you've become even more like her."

It was true. I'd always been particular about stuff, but when Austin was in the hospital that first time, that's when I'd made my deal with the universe. I'd promised to get good grades and never miss school and do all my chores, if only Austin would be okay. I'd been convinced that if I could just get everything right then nothing else would go wrong. And it had worked! Austin had recovered enough to come home, and ever since then, I'd been desperately trying to keep the universe happy.

"We can't lose sight of what's most important, okay?" Mom added.

She was right. Being there for Austin was more important than sticking with my routine. Besides, if my wish kept working, it might not matter if I veered from my schedule for one day. Just in case, though, I should probably use the rest of my spending money to get some more four-leaf clovers from Felix tomorrow.

When we got to Austin's hospital room, I was surprised to see him sitting up in bed, totally awake. Usually he was on so much pain medication the first couple of days after surgery that he'd be too groggy and cranky to do much besides watch cartoons.

"The doctor was in a little while ago and said Bug's making a miraculous recovery," Dad told us, his eyes shining.

My heart felt warm in my chest. Miraculous, or magical? Or just good karma. It didn't matter what it was. Only that it was working.

Mom busied herself scanning through Austin's chart and asking him a million questions about how he was feeling until he started trying to hide under his pillow. Sometimes she sounded like one of the doctors.

"How's it going, buddy?" I asked, giving my brother's nose a honk.

He smiled back at me. "Kinda boring. Did you feed my turtles?"

"Yup," I told him. "Those guys are pigs!"

"They're not pigs. They're *ninjas!*" he said. Then he started pretending to spin a pair of nunchucks over his head like the characters in those goofy cartoons he was always watching.

"Austin, careful of your IV!" Mom called, but she was smiling.

It was Dad's turn to head home so that he could take a shower and change, but before he went, he turned to me and said, "Oh, Lex. A boy named Elijah dropped this off for you." He handed me a paper bag. Inside were the snacks I'd accidentally left in the cafeteria along with another Batman drawing for Austin, this one of the two of them water-skiing.

When Austin saw the picture, his entire face lit up.

"I'm winning a race against Batman!" he cried. Sure enough, Elijah had drawn it so that Batman was firmly in second place. Austin was even more excited when he saw that I'd remembered to bring his Batman action figure from home.

"Who's Elijah?" Mom asked me as she settled in to read some comics with Austin and Batman.

"Just a kid from school," I said. "Actually, not anymore. He's homeschooled now. He's an artist and he doodles all over his clothes . . ." Mom's eyebrows went up, as if she thought maybe Elijah was more like a boy-boy than a friend-boy. "His mom works at the hospital, that's all."

"Mom, Mom, Mom!" Austin said. "Can you scratch behind my ears?"

Mom laughed softly and did as he asked. Austin curled up against her and kept flipping through the comic book, looking like a happy kitten.

"It's nice to see you finally making some new friends," Mom said to me.

"I thought you loved Cassa!"

"Of course I do. But you've always been so afraid of new things, Lexi. I don't want it to hold you back in life. I mean, look at your aunt! I don't want you to struggle the way she has."

I almost choked. I might have been Grandma Jean's clone, but Aunt Glinda and I couldn't be more different. When I tried to tell Mom that, she only gave me an "if you say so" look and turned back to Austin.

✳   ✳   ✳

On Friday morning, I was exhausted from staying up late studying for my math test. I had to get a good grade, especially since I'd missed a whole day of school. Just because things had been going well lately didn't mean

I could give up on my deal with the universe. It was finally holding up its end of the bargain. I couldn't start slacking now.

When I got to the footbridge, I was relieved to see Cassa waiting for me as usual. But she wasn't reading one of her history books. She was staring at the trees, nervously twisting one of her curls around her finger.

"What's wrong?" I asked.

"Oh, nothing. It's just . . . I still haven't heard from Marina. She wasn't in school yesterday, and she hasn't called or anything. I tried stopping by her house, but no one was home. I know you said she's okay, but I'm kind of worried."

"She's fine," I said. Maybe the wish I'd made *had* been a little extreme, but there was nothing I could do about it now. Even if I wanted to undo it, I wasn't sure how.

"I guess she's blowing me off." Cassa huffed. "I don't get it. We've been having fun working on our time capsule project. And we have so much stuff in common."

That last part stung, especially since it wasn't true. Marina trekked all over the world, while Cassa and her mom never traveled because they couldn't close down the antique store for too long. (And, of course, my family never went anywhere because we couldn't risk being too far away from Austin's doctors.) Besides, I was the one who'd known Cassa forever. I knew her better than anyone!

But I clenched my teeth and said, "She's probably busy or something."

"Yeah," Cassa said, but she sounded so sad. "I guess I was hoping this year would be different."

I didn't know why she'd gotten so obsessed with things changing. I wondered, suddenly, what she would have done with the wishing stones if she'd found them first. I shuddered to think what her Friendship wish might have been.

As we walked through the maze of residential streets behind the school, I was bursting to tell Cassa about the wishing stones, which were now safely tucked away in the back of my T-shirt drawer at home, but I kept my lips firmly shut. What if spilling the secret made the wish stop working?

Besides, what if she figured out that I'd also used the stones on her? I seriously doubted she'd be okay with that.

"How was the knitting club meeting?" I asked instead.

Cassa let out a soft laugh. "A disaster. I tried to make a square and it turned into a Swiss-cheese oval. I think I'll try the journalism club instead."

"Since when do you like to write?" The last time Cassa and I had worked on an English report together, I'd done most of the work.

"Well, it's not my favorite," Cassa admitted. "But who knows? It could be fun. My dad would be so excited if I told him I was going to be a writer too."

"Your dad?" I repeated in surprise. "I didn't know you even talked to him." After her parents split up, Cassa's dad had moved to the other side of the country to teach writing at some fancy college. I couldn't remember the last time she'd even mentioned him.

She shrugged. "Yeah, he's been calling every once in a while. He lives in England now, so he's been telling me about some of the historical places he's been researching for a new book."

"Wow," I said.

"I know. It sounds so cool."

But that wasn't what I meant. I thought Cassa and I told each other everything. But clearly, that wasn't true. Not anymore.

Chapter 9

The math test was going great until Mrs. Connor noticed that I was chewing gum.

"Lexi? We have a 'no gum' policy in this school, remember?" she said softly since the other kids were still working away on their tests.

"Oh, sorry," I whispered. "I just . . . I need it."

"What do you mean?" she asked. I could tell by the look on her face that she wouldn't accept anything but the truth.

"I watched a video that said if you chewed the same flavor gum while you were studying and when you were taking the test, you were guaranteed to do better, and I really want to do well on this!" I thought I'd been sneaky with my piece of juicy watermelon, but Mrs. Connor must have had super sight or smell or something. "I'll spit it out right after the test is over, I promise."

But Mrs. Connor wasn't having it. "Now, please."

"I can't," I told her. "As soon as I'm done with the test."

"You'll get rid of it *now*," she said, her voice growing louder. No one was working on the test anymore. They were all staring at me.

The taste of watermelon was suddenly sour in my mouth. What choice did I have? I got up and spit the gum out in the front of the class. Then I went back to finish my test, telling myself that it was fine. I'd still get a good grade. Austin would be okay.

At the end of class, Mrs. Connor waved me up to her desk and handed me a detention slip. My mouth dropped open. "What's this for?" I asked.

"I'm sorry, Lexi, but you were breaking the rules again. I'm surprised at you. You've been such a conscientious student so far this year."

I couldn't believe it. "But it was only gum! And I did it because—"

"Even if you had a good reason, the rules are the rules. I'm sorry." She gave me a sad smile. "Lunch detention again today, okay?"

I could only nod as I took the detention slip. "Is there any way you could grade the test now?" I asked. Otherwise I'd drive myself nuts wondering how I'd done on it.

She pulled my paper out of the pile and then hunched over it with a green pen. I bounced on my toes as I waited, crossing and uncrossing my fingers. Finally, Mrs. Connor looked up and smiled. "A ninety-six. Nice job."

It wasn't a perfect grade, but it was a really good one. Finally, I was making up some of the ground I'd lost with my previous quizzes. "Thanks," I said with a relieved sigh.

"I appreciate how hard you've been working. You've improved a lot in the past few weeks."

"I'm usually good at math," I said. "You do things differently than I'm used to."

Her smile widened. "We need to keep our minds adaptable, don't we? Math is so much more than numbers."

That reminded me of what she'd said the other day about improvement versus perfection. It sounded nice, but what good would it do if my math skills improved but Austin got worse again?

As I left the room, I practically walked into a flyer for the dance club audition. Someone had taped it to the doorframe and it brushed against my cheek as I passed by. I'd been trying to forget all about the audition, but the universe kept smacking me in the face with reminders. Maybe that meant I was supposed to listen.

❀　❀　❀

When I got to lunchtime detention, it was mostly the same kids as last time, almost like it was a club that met every day. A club I definitely didn't want to be part of for any longer than necessary.

I plopped down in the nearest desk and was surprised to see Felix sitting in the corner, his feet up on the chair in front of him. He'd always seemed so good at flying under the radar and not getting in trouble. How had he wound up here?

"Let's get started," Mrs. Connor said. I was afraid she'd force us to talk about our "patterns of behavior" again, but today she put us in pairs and asked us to chat with each other. "I want you to dig deeper about why you're really here," she instructed.

I was actually kind of glad when she put me with Felix. That way I could ask him about putting aside a few more four-leaf clovers for me before he ran out.

"What are you doing here?" I asked, going to sit in the desk next to his.

Felix smiled his innocent little smile. "The vice principal found out about my little side business."

I gasped. "Does that mean you won't be doing it anymore?"

"Relax," Felix said. "It just means I can't sell anything on school property. I'll set up shop on the other side of the school fence, that's all."

Phew. "Good, because I need to buy some more."

"Already?" he asked. "Not that I'm complaining, but that's a lot more than usual."

"I need the luck, that's all," I said. "Things have been kind of . . . complicated lately."

Felix thought for a second. Then he leaned in and said in a low voice, "Look, I probably shouldn't be saying this because it's bad for business, but maybe you're taking this whole luck thing a little too seriously."

"What do you mean?" How else was I supposed to take it? Especially when I'd literally stumbled across some lucky wishing stones?

He shrugged. "I don't know. Maybe instead of handing all your money over to me, you could figure out how to make your own luck."

Right. Easy for Felix to say when he had an uncanny ability to find four-leaf clovers wherever he went.

"I didn't think kids like you even knew how to get a detention," Felix added when I didn't say anything.

I slumped in my seat. "I'm suddenly really good at getting in trouble." Ever since the day I'd found the wishing stones, in fact. Yes, I'd only gotten two detentions, but that was two more than I'd gotten in my entire life! Almost as if the universe were trying to even itself out.

✽ ✽ ✽

I'd expected Marina never to speak to me again, so I was surprised to find her marching up to my locker before last period.

"Have you seen Cassa? She hasn't been in school."

"Um . . . yeah. She's fine," I said. Then I couldn't help adding, "I thought you weren't talking to her anymore."

"I wish," Marina said. "But we're supposed to be working on a social studies project together. It's due next week."

I sucked in a breath. The time capsule project. I'd forgotten all about it. How was Cassa supposed to get it done when she and her partner couldn't even see each other?

"Oh, um," I said. "I'll tell her you were asking about it."

Marina sighed. "Okay. Thanks, I guess." For a second, it almost looked as though there were tears in her eyes. But then she threw her shoulders back and stomped away.

After last period, Cassa was waiting for me at our usual bench. "Sorry, I'm not walking home today," I said. "I have to go to my aunt's house and wait for my dad."

"That's okay. I just came to tell you that I'm staying after for journalism club." There was something off about Cassa's voice, as if she were miles away.

"What's wrong?" I asked.

She groaned. "Marina and I are supposed to be

working on our time capsule project together, but I haven't seen her! Our class went to the library to work on it today, and I had to do a bunch of research by myself. There's no way I'll get through it all on my own in time. And we were supposed to meet tonight to work on it, but I can't even get ahold of her!"

As if I didn't already feel bad enough that my wish had stressed Cassa out. I couldn't have her failing her project because of something I did.

"Give her some time," I said. "I'm sure you'll hear from her soon." Maybe I could do some of the research and give it to Cassa and pretend it came from Marina? And then I'd have to give Cassa's research to Marina too. Ugh. This was starting to get more and more complicated.

"Really?" Cassa frowned at me. "Since when are you laid-back about anything? I figured you'd be telling me to call the FBI."

She was right. I wasn't acting like my usual self. "I

just . . . I understand why you're worried," I said, "but I'm sure the project will be fine. You still have time to figure it out."

"That's true." Cassa smiled. "Thanks, Lexi. I don't know where this more relaxed version of you came from, but I like it."

"Um, thanks," I said, but it didn't feel like a compliment.

Chapter 10

As I headed to Aunt Glinda's house, I was actually kind of excited about being there this time. I could focus on organizing my aunt's kitchen while I waited for Dad to pick me up and bring me to the hospital. That was bound to make me feel better, and the house could definitely use it.

"Look!" Aunt Glinda said when I went inside. "I got mini mason jars like you told me to, and some chalkboard labels."

The labels weren't the exact right size, but they'd do the job. We got to work emptying the spices into the jars and then carefully labeling them with chalk. Once we had them all lined up on the shelf alphabetically, they looked great.

"I hope I'll be able to keep them this neat!" my aunt said.

"You will," I reassured her, and I made a mental note to check the spices next time I came by.

"This is actually kind of fun," Aunt Glinda said. "What's next?"

"Hmm." I scanned the overwhelming collage of papers stuck to the fridge and the stacks of dusty cookbooks blocking the basement door. Then I glanced at all the pots and pans and Tupperware containers that were practically bursting out of the cupboards. That should be an easy next project. "Any chance you have some magazine holders?" I asked.

My aunt gave me a blank look. "What's a magazine holder?"

"Hmm, what about some small bins?"

She thought for a second. "I have some old shoe-boxes. Will those work?"

Probably not. "How about we start by weeding out the pans and containers you don't use anymore, and then we can figure out how to store the rest."

"Sounds good!" Aunt Glinda said. "Cleaning is much easier when you don't have to do it yourself."

Normally, I disagreed. I preferred to do things alone so that I could do them my way, but it was nice that Aunt Glinda was getting so into it. At this rate, we'd get the house back in shape in no time.

When I said that to Aunt Glinda, she laughed. "Honestly, I'm not sure the house was ever 'in shape.' Grandma Jean loved acquiring things. She'd keep them all neatly stacked everywhere, but she liked the comfort of having her things all around her." She sighed. "After she passed away, I tried to keep the house the way she had it, but it turns out I'm no good at being a neat freak. I think your mom got that gene.

I just got the gene that makes it hard for me to let go of things."

"Huh. I think maybe I got both of them," I said. But without the "acquiring things" part.

Aunt Glinda patted my shoulder. "You even smile like your grandmother sometimes. And did you know that she loved to dance too?"

"Wow, really?" I said. Then, realizing I'd sounded too eager, I added, "I never said I liked to dance." But I could tell my aunt wasn't fooled.

As we went back to sorting through endless pots and pans, I suddenly couldn't stop thinking about the dance club auditions. The club advisor, Miss Flores, had posted a video of the steps online. I'd memorized them the night before, but I hadn't had a chance to run through them over and over until they were perfect. Since the audition was on Monday, I was running out of time.

Finally, I couldn't stand it anymore. I told Aunt Glinda to keep sorting while I went to catch up on some homework. Then I locked myself in the guest room where she wouldn't see. I put music on and did the steps slowly at first, getting each one perfect. Then I did them faster and faster, until my body was moving without my brain having to tell it what to do. That was the best feeling, just moving and dancing and being part of the music. Not worrying or planning or even thinking. It was heaven.

Then I heard knocking. I quickly turned the music off and opened the door.

"Practicing?" Aunt Glinda asked. She was smiling in triumph.

"Um, maybe." I didn't want her getting her hopes up about the audition since there was a very good chance I'd chicken out again.

"Your friend is here," she said.

"Cassa?" Maybe she'd changed her mind about going to the journalism club.

"No, that boy. Eli or something? I've seen him riding his skateboard around the neighborhood."

"Oh, Elijah." What was he doing here?

I found him perched on the front porch, sketching a wolf face on the left knee of his jeans with a Sharpie. "Hey," he said when he saw me. "What's up?" I saw a flash of gum in his mouth that was as blue as his glasses.

"How did you know I was going to be here today?" I asked.

"I live right over there," he said, pointing past some trees. "I saw you walking this way. Is that your aunt?"

I nodded.

"There used to be this crazy old lady who lived here," he said. "She never talked to anyone and one time I saw her sitting in the middle of the lawn, cutting it with scissors."

"That was my grandmother," I said flatly. "She wasn't crazy. She was just . . . particular."

Elijah laughed. "Ah, so that's where you get it from."

There was something about his laugh that made my annoyance disappear. Because let's face it, the more I found out about my grandmother, the more I realized that she and I were the same brand of odd. But Elijah didn't seem to mind.

He blew a big blue bubble and then said, "So listen, I was thinking you could help me with my hospital project."

"But I can't draw."

"That's okay. It's figuring out what to say in the cards that's the hard part. I thought you might know what sick kids want to hear. Like if anything will actually make them feel better."

"I don't know. Austin just liked that someone was thinking of him. It doesn't really matter what you write."

"Oh," he said, sounding genuinely disappointed. Huh. Did he really want my help that badly?

"But I can try to come up with something, if you want," I found myself saying.

His face instantly lit up. "Cool. Want to work on it now?"

"I can't. My dad's picking me up soon."

"How about tomorrow?"

"I'm going to visit Austin during the day, and then Cassa and I usually hang out on Saturday nights." It would finally be the two of us again. I couldn't wait.

"I forgot," Elijah said. "You and Cassa are like twins, right?"

"I mean, we don't do *everything* together." Not anymore, anyway. "But yeah, we're best friends."

Elijah nodded, but he looked disappointed again. Maybe he was wishing he had a best friend too. Come to think of it, I couldn't remember Elijah having any close friends. He'd had a group of kids he'd hung out with when he still went to my school, but I never saw him with any one person. Maybe, like with everything else, he didn't worry about it.

"I'm around on Sunday afternoon if you want to work on the cards then," I offered.

Elijah beamed. "Sure!"

I expected him to ride away on his skateboard, but instead he plopped down next to me on the porch steps and said, "So what do you want to do until your dad comes?"

Um, okay. I guess we were hanging out now.

"I don't know." I was itching to go back to practicing the dance routine, but it would be rude to blow him off. Plus, I liked being around Elijah. He seemed so relaxed all the time that I didn't worry so much when I was with him.

"Do your toes ever stop tapping?" he asked with a laugh.

I glanced down and realized that my feet *were* moving on their own. "Yes," I said. "I just . . . I have a song stuck in my head."

"What song?"

"You probably wouldn't know it. It's from a musical, for this audition I'm thinking of doing at school."

Of course, once I said that, Elijah wouldn't let it go until I told him about the audition. How did he get me to open up to him like that?

"Okay, Block. Let's see some of your moves," Elijah said, leaning back on the steps.

"Nope! No way."

"If you're going to dance in public, you need to practice, don't you?"

"And what? You're going to coach me? Are you a dance expert or something?"

He shrugged. "No, but dancing is like skateboarding. You do a move a bunch of times until you get it right. So let's see what you've got."

That was true. Still, I wasn't going to dance in front of him, no matter how at ease I felt around him, so I shook my head.

"Okay, then," he said, getting to his feet. "You tell me the moves and I'll do them."

"Um, what?"

"It'll be fun, like reverse practicing. If you know the steps, then you should be able to describe how to do them, and I'll try to follow your instructions."

"If you really want to, sure." To my surprise, he nodded eagerly. Wow. He was actually serious. All right. I supposed any type of practice would be good. "Well . . . the first one is shuffle to the left, shimmy, and spin."

Elijah scrunched up his face. "What's that mean?"

"You know, a shuffle," I said. But he still looked clueless. I tried to explain how to do it, but when he followed what I said, he only looked like a dizzy zombie.

I groaned and got to my feet. "Like this!" I said, giving him the tiniest of demonstrations.

"Oh, okay." He did it, and it actually looked pretty good. "And then what? A shinny? Like you climb something?"

"No, a *shimmy*. You know, where you kind of shake your shoulders."

He moved his shoulders up and down in the most ridiculous way.

"No!" I said, laughing. "Like this!" I gave him another demonstration. And then I realized: He'd tricked me! He was making me dance. But the weird thing was, I actually didn't mind.

"And now a spin," I added. "Like this." I did my most dramatic twirl and glanced over at Elijah, who was standing back looking impressed.

"Not bad, Block," he said. "You really know what you're doing."

My cheeks were hot and I was kind of mortified that I'd actually let Elijah see me dance, but I had to admit it was nice to know that I wasn't completely terrible.

I might have even shown him a few more steps if my dad's car hadn't pulled up just then.

"Oops, gotta go," I said.

"All right," Elijah said. "But you're not getting out of this that easily. You'll have to show me the routine another time."

"Maybe," I said with a laugh. "If you're lucky."

Chapter 11

Normally, on Saturday mornings, I would do homework and watch life hack videos or—when no one else
was home—choreograph dances to my favorite songs.
But that morning, it was back to the hospital. The place
was starting to feel like a second home but definitely
not in a good way.

The minute Dad and I stepped into my brother's
room, though, Mom announced that Austin had a clean
bill of health. All we needed to do was wait for his dis-
charge papers, and we could go home.

"No one can believe it," Mom said. "The doctors thought about keeping him for one more day, just to be on the safe side . . . but I mean, look at him!"

Austin was darting around the tiny room, pretending to use an imaginary grappling hook Batman-style. He'd been almost back to his old self when we'd visited the day before, but this was unbelievable. He didn't look as though he'd ever been sick.

"Careful," Mom called as Austin tried to jump onto a chair. "You don't want to rip your stitches." But her voice wasn't all high-pitched anymore, and she went back to chatting with Dad instead of lasering in on Austin's every move with worried eyes.

Soon, we were all piling into the car and heading home. I kept sneaking glances at Austin, trying to see if he was glowing or anything because of my wish. But he looked normal. No too-pale face. No bloated stomach. No complaints that he wasn't feeling well. He was just Austin.

When we got home, Austin instantly asked for some celery sticks, which made my mom beam. Normally, it was a challenge to get him to eat anything that didn't come in a wrapper.

He chomped into a piece of celery and asked, "Can I go play in the yard?"

My parents exchanged uneasy looks. I could tell they were feeling the same way I was: relieved to see Austin acting so full of energy, but worried that something would happen and we'd wind up right back in the hospital.

"Only for a few minutes," Mom said.

"Then we'll set you up on the couch for the afternoon, and you can watch some movies. Okay, Bug?" Dad added.

Austin didn't seem thrilled about having to rest more after spending the past few days in bed, but he nodded and ran to the back door, waiting to be let out like an impatient puppy.

"Can you go keep an eye on him, Lexi?" Mom asked. "Your dad and I have some things to sort out."

By "things" I knew she meant bills. My parents always tried to send me out of earshot when it was time to argue about money.

When we went outside, I expected Austin to head over to his favorite spot by the fence where Batman was always climbing up to save a variety of action figures. But this time, Austin went over to the recycling bin and pulled out some newspapers.

He carried the stack over to the sandbox that he barely used anymore, then pulled off the cover and spread the newspapers all over the sand.

"What are you doing?" I asked.

"Playing."

I perched on one of the swings and watched him arranging and rearranging the papers, as if he were trying to put them into some kind of order. It wasn't his usual kind of game, but Austin's imagination was always going. You never knew what he'd think of next.

After a minute, when Austin was so busy that he wasn't even looking in my direction, I checked to make sure my parents couldn't see me out the window. Then I started practicing my dance routine.

I was whirling and twirling, counting the steps and humming the music to myself, when I suddenly heard my parents' voices coming from the kitchen. A lot louder than usual.

I stopped dancing and strained to hear. Something about "not enough in the account," which had to mean money.

"We haven't even paid off the bills from last time," Mom said.

And then Dad, who was usually so laid-back about everything, replied, "I don't know how much longer we can keep going like this."

It was about Austin, of course. It always was. Just a second ago my head had been spinning with the joy of dancing, but now I only felt dizzy. I wished there was something I could do. Why couldn't I have found those stones earlier? I glanced at Austin, who was now shredding the newspaper into long strips, smiling the whole time.

He was finally healthy. Everything else would work itself out. It had to.

❄   ❄   ❄

On Saturday nights, Cassa and I would usually hang out in her basement. But when Dad dropped me off at her house, her mom waved me through the almost-remodeled kitchen, which still needed a few cabinet doors, and sent me upstairs instead. Cassa was on her bed, scrolling through what looked like newspaper articles on her laptop.

"What are you doing?" I asked.

"Oh, nothing," she said absently. Then she glanced at the papers tucked awkwardly under my arm. "What's that?"

"Um, Marina gave me some of her research to give you for your project."

"Really?" Cassa grabbed the papers and started scanning through them. I'd spent hours the night before looking up everything I could about the 1960s and writing down what I thought should go in the time capsule. I thought I'd done a pretty good job until Cassa tossed the papers on the floor and cried, "I can't believe it. Does she want us to fail?"

"Huh?"

"Who cares about 1960s *America*? We're supposed to be focusing on England!"

I stared at her. Had I done all that work for nothing?

"When did she give you these?" Cassa asked. "When did you see her?"

"I didn't. She dropped them off at my house yesterday. She left them on our doorstep." Yes, it was a lie, but at least it was less of a lie than saying that I had actually spoken to Marina.

"I knew it!" Cassa cried. "There's something strange going on." Then she turned back to the laptop. "I've been trying to figure out how to file a missing persons report."

"Like with the police?"

"Yes!" Cassa whirled around. Her eyes looked a little wild. "I know you said I shouldn't worry, but something happened to Marina. I just know it! You should have seen how weird her mom was acting when I went over there this morning."

"Wait, you talked to her mom? What happened?"

"Marina wasn't home! And she hasn't been in school for days. When I asked her mom about it, she acted like she had no idea what I was talking about. Then she started talking to someone, even though there was no one there. I think she's crazy, Lexi. I bet she locked Marina up in the basement or sold her to the circus or something!"

"Sold her to the circus?" I repeated.

"Look at this article!" Cassa cried, pointing to the laptop. "Some girl disappeared, and months later the police found her doing the high dive in a circus act."

I strained to read over her shoulder. "That article also looks like it was from about a hundred years ago. I don't even think circuses do high dive acts anymore."

But Cassa wasn't listening. "I know how this all sounds! But something happened to Marina. Maybe something bad! Not only are we going to fail our social studies project but I might never see her again!"

Okay, I had to tell her the truth. Even though she'd hate me. Even though it might mess up the wish. I couldn't have my best friend thinking that Marina had been murdered or something!

"This is my fault," I said.

"No, it's not," Cassa said. "I mean, you haven't exactly been friendly to Marina, but there's something else going on."

"I know. That's what I'm trying to tell you." I had to just blurt it out. All of it. "I found some wishing stones at the antique shop, and I made a wish, and I wished that you and Marina would stop being friends, only I worded it wrong, and now you guys can't see each other, and I'm really sorry, and I didn't know it would mess up your social studies project or make you so upset and stuff."

I stopped talking and sucked in a breath, realizing that I'd spilled it all so fast, there was a chance Cassa hadn't even been able to understand me.

She stared at me for a long minute. And then she closed her eyes. "Just . . . stop it, Lexi."

"What do you mean?"

She opened her eyes again, and they were suddenly angry slits. "I can't believe you'd make fun of me when I'm freaking out."

"Make fun of you? What are you talking about?"

"Look, I know you don't believe in any of that magic stuff that I'm always talking about, but you don't have to make a joke of it. I get it. You don't like Marina."

"Th-that's not what I'm saying!" I cried.

But Cassa only shook her head and said, "Maybe you should go so I can work on my project. I'll call you tomorrow, okay?"

I guess I didn't have a choice. I went downstairs and called my mom to pick me up. Then I waited in the semi-chaotic kitchen by myself, surrounded by a mess of tools and boxes and tarps. I was so busy trying not to cry that I didn't even have the urge to organize them.

Chapter 12

Sunday morning was a blur of catching up on homework, nervously watching Austin every second to make sure he was okay, and trying to forget the scene with Cassa the night before. I was actually relieved when it was time to head over to Elijah's house in the afternoon to work on cards for the kids at the hospital.

My mom was more than happy to give me a ride. I could tell she was excited that I was hanging out with someone new. As we drove through Elijah's neighborhood, Mom smiled to herself.

"It's funny that I grew up around here and now I almost never go to this part of town." She pointed across the street. "I remember I used to hide in those bushes over there."

"You, hiding?" I asked. That didn't sound like her.

"I think I was in there planning how I would take over the world. I was going to become a doctor and travel everywhere and lead an exciting life."

"So why didn't you?"

"Oh, priorities change. I met your father and we wanted to start a family. It made more sense for me to go work for a drug company than to go to medical school. And then after you were born and we started trying to have a second baby, well, that became the main focus." After Austin had been born, Mom had quit her full-time job and started working part-time at a clothing store, which had a lot more flexible hours but also paid a lot less.

"I don't regret any of it," Mom quickly added. "Family is the most important thing."

And yet, Mom barely hung out with her sister. I'd never really thought about that before, not until I'd started spending more time with my aunt. "Mom, why do we never see Aunt Glinda?"

She blinked at me in surprise. "You were just at her house."

"No, I mean all of us. Why do we only do holidays together?"

Mom thought for a minute. "I suppose . . . well, it's no secret that Glinda and I have never been very alike. I've always been focused on the next big thing in my life. Your aunt is . . . she's not like that. She lives in the past."

"But it makes her sad," I said, remembering how I'd found her crying at her kitchen table the other day.

"I think sometimes it's easy to feel that life has left you behind, you know? My sister has always done the safe thing: staying at the same job, not moving away from home, avoiding meeting new people. And everything around her has changed."

When I thought about it like that, no wonder my aunt seemed so emotional all the time. Maybe wanting to get rid of the clutter in her house meant she was finally ready to change too.

We pulled up to Elijah's house, and I hopped out. I told myself there was no reason to be nervous, but there was an unpleasant jumpy feeling in my stomach.

"Have fun!" Mom called with a knowing smile.

"Hey, come in," Elijah said when I knocked on the door, as if I came over all the time. As if we'd been friends forever. The nerves I'd been feeling started to melt away.

"Wait," I said, pausing dramatically at the door. "You're not going to trick me into dancing again, are you?"

He snorted. "No. But maybe one of these days I'll find a way to get you on a skateboard." He waved me through the house, putting his finger to his lips. "Mama Ann's working in her studio upstairs. We have to be quiet until she comes down."

"Is she an artist like you?" I whispered.

"She makes jewelry. She's really good. People buy tons of her stuff online."

I couldn't help thinking of the beaded necklaces Marina was always making and how much she'd love to meet a real jewelry designer. Maybe if things ever calmed down, I could introduce the two of them or something. Then again, Marina would probably turn around and try to steal Elijah from me too.

We went outside and crossed the backyard, and then we came to a small yellow shed. Elijah opened the door, and I gasped at the little artist studio inside.

"Is this yours?" I asked.

"Yup," he said. "I set it up last year. It gets pretty cold in the winter, but otherwise it's awesome." He pointed me to an old metal folding chair, and I plopped down, admiring the sketches all over the walls. Instead of a drawing table, Elijah had a couple of sawhorses with a plank of wood on top, and there were plastic milk crates instead of shelves. Coffee mugs crammed with pencils and brushes and tubes of paint were scattered all around. The place was messy and colorful and chaotic. I wasn't sure I could stand to be in here for hours on end, but it was perfect for Elijah.

He handed me a few of the drawings he'd made and I got to work coming up with messages to write on them. It was surprising how comfortable I was around him considering we barely knew each other. Even when we'd gone to school together, we hadn't talked much. He'd been the quiet kid in the back of the room who was always scribbling in a sketchbook. He was still kind of quiet, but in a good way.

"How's your brother doing?" he asked after a while.

"Good," I said, and it was strange to say it and actually mean it. "He's recovering a lot faster than anyone thought he would. And he's gotten really into crunching on veggies, for some reason. Cucumbers and carrots and even broccoli! My parents think it's an extreme reaction to eating hospital food for so long."

Elijah laughed. "He's a lucky kid."

"Lucky? Are you serious? He's had nothing but bad luck since he was born. It's like all I can do to try to make up for it."

"No, I mean he's lucky to have you looking out for him." He gave me a curious look. "What do you mean you've been trying to make up for it?"

"I . . . I have a deal with the universe," I said. And then, even though I knew he wouldn't understand, I went ahead and told him about my balance theory.

"Huh," he said when I was done. "Cool."

"You're not going to laugh at me? Or tell me I'm a weirdo?"

"Why would I do that?"

"Because . . . because people never understand. They think I'm crazy for doing all that stuff to help Austin."

"It makes you feel better to do it, right?" he asked.

"Yeah, I guess. At least it made makes me feel like I can do *something* instead of waiting around and hoping things will work out." Maybe Felix could do that when he was sitting on a mound of four-leaf clovers, but it was definitely not my style.

"Then who cares what anyone else thinks?" Elijah asked.

And that was the end of the conversation. I didn't have to burn with shame the way I had with Marina.

"Hey, can you hand me the cerulean?" Elijah asked after a minute.

I stared at him. "The what?"

He pointed to one of the colored pencils. "That one."

"You mean the *blue*?"

"Yeah, I guess you can call it that." He laughed as I passed it to him. "It's more of an azure anyway."

I rolled my eyes. "If you say so."

As we kept working, I felt myself relaxing, really relaxing, for the first time in what felt like forever. When it was time to leave, I was kind of bummed to go. Especially when I got into Mom's car and I could tell by the way she kept clicking her tongue and shaking her head as she drove that her mind was far away.

"How's Austin doing?" I asked, because that's how most of our conversations started these days.

She blinked. "Oh, he's great. He spent all afternoon working on some 'top secret project' in his room, which involved a lot of construction paper. And he found some old sippy cup from when he was a baby and started drinking water from it."

"A sippy cup?"

Mom shook her head. "I don't ask. As long as he's staying hydrated, I'm happy."

As we pulled into our driveway, Mom's phone rang. I could tell by the way her mouth pulled down at the edges when she answered it that it wasn't good news. "We're working on it," she told the person on the other end. "We'll figure out another payment plan."

My stomach clenched back into its usual fist. Money again. It always came back to that. Even though having Austin healthy should have made all our lives perfect, they weren't. It wasn't fair. Even with supposedly magical wishing stones, things still weren't right!

When we got inside, I went up to my room to look at the stones again. I'd already used the Health and Friendship ones. That left Success and Family. I wondered if I should use them to make wishes about my family succeeding in winning the lottery or something—but then I thought of the mess with Cassa and Marina. Maybe it would be best not to use them at all, at least for now.

Still, I tucked the wishing stones back into my backpack. Just in case.

✽　✽　✽

In the morning, Cassa was waiting at the footbridge, but she didn't say much on the way to school. I didn't dare bring up the whole Marina situation. I couldn't tell if she was mad at me after our sort-of fight on Saturday, and I was afraid to ask.

"What's that?" I asked, noticing a big manila envelope tucked under her arm as we turned onto the school walkway.

"Nothing," she said.

More silence. Ugh. What happened to us? We used to babble the whole way to school, even though we never had anything all that important to say to each other. Now that there was so much to talk about, we couldn't say a word.

"I didn't get a chance to ask you how the journalism club was the other day," I finally said.

Cassa groaned. "Do you know how much writing they want you to do every week? No way. Not for me. But there's a fencing club starting up, so I might try that."

Fencing? Really? Cassa complained if she had to wear goggles at the pool. I couldn't picture her putting on all that equipment. But I didn't say anything since she'd probably bite my head off about it.

"Hey," she went on. "Aren't the dance auditions starting today?"

"Oh, right," I said, as if I hadn't been up half the night stressing about them. Before she could pester me about auditioning, I threw out, "Guess who I saw yesterday? Elijah Lewis-Green. Remember him? We're working on a project together."

Cassa stopped walking. "A project? But he's not in school with us anymore, is he?"

"No. It's not a school project. I kind of bumped into him at the hospital the other day and he asked me to help him with something."

"So you guys are like friends now?" Cassa asked, and for some reason she sounded mad.

"I guess so. It's not a big deal."

Cassa let out a strange laugh. "Are you serious? You're like the world's worst person at making new friends, and suddenly you've been hanging out with Elijah and you didn't even tell me?"

"Since when do I need to check with you before I make new friends?" Cassa certainly hadn't done that when she'd brought Marina into our group.

"That—that's not what I'm saying!" Cassa cried. "God, Lexi. Sometimes you can be so clueless!" Then she marched off ahead of me toward the school.

And maybe I *was* clueless, because I didn't get it. The two of us had always been best friends. Why were things suddenly so hard?

Then I remembered what my mom had said about me being like my aunt. Aunt Glinda who avoided making new friends and trying new things and spent most of her time alone. No. That was stupid. I was never going to wind up like her.

When I got to school, I kept seeing flyers for the dance club audition everywhere. *Today after school! First round of dance auditions!* There was even one taped to my locker.

"Okay, universe," I muttered to myself. "I get it. I'll try out, okay?"

And part of me was actually excited about the idea. But by lunchtime, I was starting to freak out about all the things that could go wrong. So, instead of going to the cafeteria, I headed off to the bathroom with the bag of wishing stones clenched in my hand. I locked myself in a stall, took out the Success stone, and stared at it for a long time. I tried to think of the perfect wording for the wish, but my head was swimming with possibilities.

Eventually, I closed my eyes tight and whispered, "I wish that I could finally succeed at performing in public."

Chapter 13

After I'd made the wish, I didn't feel any different. So, still safely locked in the bathroom stall, I tested out a few dance moves, humming the audition song under my breath as I went. I felt good. Actually, I felt great. The wish had to be working because I was suddenly sure that I was going to nail that audition!

Still, I spent the rest of lunch running through the steps in the bathroom, just in case. Even though Cassa and I hadn't eaten together in days, I was in no rush to see her after she'd practically yelled at me that morning. Besides, I was so jittery with nerves that I wouldn't be able to eat before the audition anyway.

For the rest of the day, I focused on doing everything perfectly, racking up enough good energy so that the universe would have to let my audition go well. As much as I wanted to trust that the wishing stones would take care of everything for me, we didn't exactly have a perfect track record.

By the time the final bell rang, I was feeling pretty confident. I'd aced my science quiz and answered two questions right during English and even helped a girl in the hallway find a lost water bottle that had rolled behind a trash can. Everything was set for my audition.

When I got to the auditorium, there were already a bunch of kids there running through the steps. So many kids. How was I ever going to get through to the second round of auditions next week? But I made myself take a deep breath and go write my name on the sign-up sheet. Then I went to a corner of the auditorium and did some stretches just like I'd seen in a YouTube video: jogging in place first, then doing some arm circles, knee bends, and torso twists.

After a minute, the door opened again and Marina walked in. Ugh. What was she doing here? Wasn't it bad enough that she'd tried to steal my best friend? Now she was going to try to steal my spot in the dance club?

No way was I going to let that happen.

"Okay, everybody!" Miss Flores called out. "Let's get started. I'll put you into groups and each group will get up onstage and audition together. Let's begin!"

She called out several names that didn't include mine. I went to sit in the audience to watch the first round, which included Marina. As the music started and she began doing the steps, I had to admit that she was pretty good. Her limbs were long and graceful, and the fact that she was taller than most of the other kids made your eye immediately go to her. No doubt she'd make it to the next round. She seemed to know it too, because when the routine ended, she came off the stage with a big smile on her face. Ugh.

After Miss Flores had marked a few things on her clipboard, another group of kids went up onstage. And another. Finally, there were only five kids left.

"If I haven't called your name yet, come on up!" Miss Flores said.

I could barely feel my legs as I went up the steps. How could I dance when my legs were numb? I took a spot toward the back of the stage, hoping to hide a little bit, and tried to remember how to breathe. Was it in through the nose and out through the mouth? Or vice versa? Or maybe you were only supposed to do mouth and not nose. Or was it only nose? Why couldn't I remember?

Just when I was really starting to panic, the music came on. "Five, six, seven, eight!" Miss Flores called.

My feet started moving to the music. My arms followed along. I shuffled and shimmied and turned. I hummed the song under my breath, which somehow helped me focus. I was doing it. I was really doing it!

The more into it I got, the louder my humming became. Until the kids around me started giving me weird looks, and I realized I wasn't just humming, I was singing. Belting, really. And I couldn't stop.

Even when the dance was over and everyone else had stopped moving, I was standing in the middle of the stage, singing at the top of my lungs. The craziest thing of all was that it wasn't the audition song anymore. It was a song I didn't even know, one about a girl named Sally. Who on earth was Sally?

"Thank you!" Miss Flores called out to me. But I still kept going. I tried clapping my hand over my mouth, but the song leaked through my fingers like it was determined to get out.

Miss Flores was searching through her clipboard. "Alexandra," she called out. "That's enough! You can stop now!"

Finally, I did stop. Not because she'd told me to, but because the song I'd been singing was mercifully over.

The entire auditorium was silent for a second. Then someone snickered, and I could have sworn it was Marina. I hurried off the stage, not daring to look at anyone. As I went to get my bag, I could feel everyone's laughing eyes on me.

"All right," Miss Flores called out. "I'll post the list for the final audition by Wednesday. If you don't make it to the next round, don't get discouraged and please try out again next year."

But of course, there was no way I was making it to the next round or even thinking about trying out next fall. Not after I'd totally embarrassed myself in front of everyone. I'd had my chance, and I'd blown it.

❋　❋　❋

When Aunt Glinda picked me up, she must have sensed that the audition had been a disaster because she didn't say much. She only gave me a little pat on the leg when we pulled into my driveway and said, "Win or lose, I'm glad you played the game." I guess that was supposed to make me feel better, but of course it didn't.

When I went inside, my mom was nowhere to be found. Neither was Austin. After a minute, I heard a squeaking sound coming from upstairs. Was there a mouse running loose somewhere? Maybe that's why no one was around. Mom was terrified of mice. She'd probably run out of the house screaming at the first sign of it.

Then I heard her voice upstairs. "Honey, what is all this?"

"Mom?" I called, but she didn't answer. I cautiously went up the stairs, as the squeaking got louder and louder. What *was* that?

When I got to Austin's room and pushed open the door, I gasped. The entire room was covered in shredded paper of every color imaginable—heaps of it on his bed, all over the carpet, and even spilling out of his dresser drawers. And in the corner behind his desk, curled up in what looked like a paper nest, was Austin.

"Honey," Mom said again, standing in the middle of the room with her hands on her hips. I could tell she was trying not to sound mad. "I'm glad you're feeling better, but did you have to make such a mess?"

"Squeak," said Austin. "Squeak, squeak."

Mom glanced at me. "Oh, Lex. There you are. Any idea what game this is?"

I couldn't answer. All I could do was stare at Austin, who was now drinking out of his old sippy cup, which he'd taped to the side of his desk upside down, licking it with his tongue like he was some kind of rodent at the pet store.

Austin had always had a big imagination, but this was different. Scary, almost.

Mom sighed. "All right, I need to go make some calls. Can you try to get him to clean this up, Lex?" Then she gave me a hard look. "Are you okay?"

"What? I'm fine." Maybe for a second I'd thought about telling her about my disastrous audition, but that was nothing compared to whatever was going on with Austin.

When she was gone, I slowly went over to my brother. "Austin?" I said softly. "Are you okay?"

"Squeak," he said, giving me a big smile.

"Are you . . . is this a game or . . ."

He started licking his hands as if they were paws and rubbing them over his face like a cat cleaning itself.

I swallowed and put my hand on his shoulder. He burrowed into me, nestling against my leg as if wanting me to scratch the top of his head.

As I petted his hair, reassuring him that everything would be all right, my brain was spinning. Was this another side effect from my wish? Austin's body might have been healed, but maybe he wasn't healthy after all.

Chapter 14

That night, Austin insisted on eating his dinner from a bowl on the floor. I expected my parents to be as worried about him as I was, but they still thought it was one of Austin's games. Besides, they were too busy talking about money again—or lack of it—to pay much attention.

"If I could find a better job," Dad was saying, not for the first time, "we'd be all right."

"Maybe I can try to up my hours at the store," Mom said, "you know, once everything calms down." She glanced at Austin, and I knew she meant once they were sure he was okay.

My parents talked about money the way they talked about Austin. All "what-ifs" and "maybes." The words sounded heavy coming out of their mouths.

After my brother went to bed, squeaking good night to everyone, I went up to my room to finish my homework. But all I could do was think about the wishes and how wrong they'd all gone.

A few minutes later, Mom knocked on the door. "There's a phone call for you," she said. "Elijah. Don't stay up too late, okay?"

When I picked up the phone, I was suddenly nervous, realizing that I'd pretty much only talked to Cassa on the phone before. But Elijah sounded so glad to talk to me that my nerves melted away.

"Hey, I wanted to tell you that the cards are all done thanks to you. Mama Dee's going to bring them to all the kids at the hospital tomorrow. A couple of the patients were already sent home, so I guess we did some of the cards for nothing, but I figure they're not in the hospital anymore, so it all works out, you know?"

"Um, yeah," I said. "That's good." Austin was home from the hospital, but that didn't mean he was okay. I wondered what the doctors would say if we told them what was happening. Would they have us bring him back in?

"Hey, are you all right?" Elijah asked.

"Um, I . . ." Because suddenly I wasn't, not really. Even though I wasn't sure what the rules of the wishes were, I was desperate to tell someone what was going on. Because what if there was something really wrong with Austin and it was my fault?

Before I knew it, I was spilling everything, about Cassa and Marina, about Austin, and about what had happened at my audition. And all about the wishes. When I was done, there was a long silence on the other end of the line and I wondered if Elijah had realized that he was talking to a crazy person and hung up the phone.

Then I heard him let out a long breath and say, "Wow. That's nuts. So what are we going to do?"

"We?" I repeated.

"Yeah, I mean, if you want my help, that is."

The surprising thing was, I did want his help, even though I'd always kind of done stuff on my own. Because this felt too big to handle by myself.

"Okay," I said. "Then I guess we need a plan."

❋   ❋   ❋

I saw the flyers the minute I got to school in the morning. *Missing!* they screamed in giant letters above a black-and-white picture of Marina. They were taped above water fountains, next to lockers, and on doorways. *Have you seen this girl? Call or text with any information.* At the bottom was Cassa's name and phone number.

Oh. My. God.

I started to tear them down, even though there was no way I could get them all. These must have been in the envelope Cassa had brought to school yesterday. No, no, no. This couldn't be happening!

Kids were giving the flyers confused looks at they passed or smirking as if they thought they were a joke. I kept ripping them down until I heard Cassa's voice behind me. "Lexi, stop! What are you doing?"

She ran up to me and yanked the flyers out of my hands. "Are you insane?" she said. "Do you know how long it took me to hang those?"

"You can't leave these up, Cassa. People will think Marina's really missing."

"She is!" Cassa cried. "Why won't anyone believe me?" She took out her phone. "I've already gotten a few leads. A couple of them were obviously hoaxes, though. Like someone sent a mean message saying, 'Duh. She's standing in front of you.' Can you believe that?"

I could, of course. But that was about the only thing I could believe. How had this all gotten so out of control?

"Lexi!" I heard someone yell from down the hall. I turned to find a furious-looking Marina charging toward me. "Where is she? Where's Cassa?"

I had no idea what to say. For a second, I thought about blurting out, "She's right next to you," and making a run for it.

"Why would Cassa do this?" Marina asked, motioning to the flyers all around us. "What kind of psycho thinks of something like that?"

"Lexi? What's wrong?" Cassa said. "Why do you look so freaked out?"

"I—I'm sorry," I stammered, looking back and forth between Cassa and Marina.

"For what?" they both said in unison.

"I just am," I said. "I'll fix this, somehow. I promise." Then I really did turn and run.

Chapter 15

Elijah was already waiting for me outside the school after the final bell.

"Ready to head to the Antique Barn?" he asked.

We'd decided last night that the first step in fixing Austin and getting the Cassa mess under control was figuring out where the wishing stones had come from, which meant that Elijah would come to work with me. Since Cassa had the fencing club meeting today, she wouldn't be at the shop anyway. Which was probably a good thing, considering how weird she'd acted when she'd found out that Elijah and I had been hanging out.

As we started to walk through town, I filled Elijah in on what had happened with the flyers. Then I told him how I'd spent the whole lunch period at the school library researching wishing stones. It was funny that after years of eating lunch together, Cassa and I hadn't even been in the cafeteria at the same time for the past week. But if I could figure out where the stones had come from and how to fix my wishes, maybe things with Cassa would finally go back to some sort of normal.

"I didn't find much," I told him. "One thing I read said that wishing stones come from the seashore and have to have an unbroken ring of quartz in them, but mine are definitely not made out of quartz. I also found info about wishing stones in Ireland, but we can't exactly go search there. A lot of the other stuff I read talked about wishing wells, but that doesn't help us either."

Elijah thoughtfully pushed his glasses up his nose. "Tell me again about when you found the stones."

"They came in with a bunch of old stuff on the same day someone was selling a couple of armoires."

"So they were used," Elijah said.

"Used?"

"If they were with other old stuff, maybe whoever owned them in the first place already used them."

Used wishes? Was it even possible to use wishes more than once? Then again, was *any* of this possible?

"If they were already used, maybe the wish wasn't as strong as it should have been and that's why things have been going haywire," I said.

"I don't know," Elijah said, looking doubtful. "Based on everything you told me, the wish seemed pretty strong to me."

"Then why are things going so wrong? I never wished for Austin to start acting crazy, and I definitely wasn't looking to turn my dance audition into my Broadway debut!" *A Broadway debut . . .* I stopped walking. "But wait—what if the first person was?"

"On Broadway?" Elijah asked.

"No, what if whoever owned the wishing stones before me used the Success wish to be good at singing?

So when I used the stone again, my wish came true, but part of someone else's wish did too."

"Okay, but what about Austin? What did the other person use the Health stone for that would make him act all nuts?"

"I don't know. Maybe a squirrel fell out of a tree or something and the person used the stone to save its life." And somehow that had made Austin start acting like a squirrel—or whatever he was—too.

Elijah was nodding, as if this all made sense. Maybe it did, in some twisted sort of way. "But what about Cassa?" he asked. "You wanted her and Marina to stop talking and seeing each other. That wish seemed to go okay."

"I don't know," I admitted. Technically Elijah was right. I'd gotten exactly what I'd wished for with the Friendship wish. Of course, I should have wished for Cassa to be my best friend again, rather than trying to get Marina out of the picture. But that wasn't the wishing stone's fault. That was mine.

"Maybe the first person wished for the same thing," Elijah said.

"They wished for Cassa and Marina not to be friends anymore?" I asked with a laugh.

"Well, no. Obviously not. But something similar enough that it didn't warp your wish the way the other ones did."

"Maybe," I said, but it sounded like too much of a coincidence. Still, things were finally starting to add up. "If that's all true, how do we fix this? I want my brother to be healthy, *really* healthy. When I left the house, he'd put one of the outdoor trash cans on its side and was trying to run around inside it, like a gerbil or something."

Elijah chuckled, and yeah, maybe it was kind of funny when it wasn't happening to your little brother. "I don't know," he admitted. "But figuring out who the stones belonged to will help."

When we got to the Antique Barn, Ms. Hinkley was clearly surprised to see me there with a stranger at my side. "What have you done to my daughter?" she joked.

"This is Elijah," I said as he reached out and politely shook Ms. Hinkley's hand. "We wanted to ask you a question."

"Oh, sure."

"I found a bag of stones in one of the boxes you had me sort through last week, and I kept them. Now I'm trying to figure out who they belonged to. Any chance they came in with those armoires?"

Ms. Hinkley frowned. "No, I don't think so. I'm pretty sure I was having you unpack the boxes that someone left on our steps."

That's what I'd been afraid of. "So the stones could have come from anyone?"

"I guess so." I must have looked upset because Ms. Hinkley asked, "Is everything all right?"

"I just need to find the person who owned them before. It's important."

She thought for a second. "Well, I can give you the inventory list for the things we put on the shelves that day. Maybe something there will help."

I thought of the things I'd sorted through, of the calendars and ratty T-shirts and concert tickets I'd put aside. Those might have helped tell us who they'd belonged to, but they'd all gone in the trash.

Still, Elijah and I got to work going through the inventory list and then tracking down the items on the shelves. When we were finished, we had a pile of dishes and cutlery, stacks of old cassette tapes, and a couple of salt and pepper shakers.

"Not sure a bunch of tapes is going to help us," Elijah said when we'd finished looking at all the items. He flipped through a few of them. "All grunge bands. Mama Dee was into this stuff when she was our age. She tried to get me to listen to it once, but . . ." He shrugged. "I don't know. It was weird to think about either of my moms being in middle school, you know? It made my brain hurt."

I laughed, trying to imagine my parents at my age. All I could picture was them stressing out about lunch money. It was funny to think that they hadn't even known

151

each other back then. Mom had grown up in town, but she hadn't met Dad until she'd gone away to college.

"Look!" Elijah said, pointing to one of the tapes. On it someone had written: *For Gem.*

"Gem?" I repeated. "Who names their kid Gem?"

"Isn't your aunt's name Glinda?" Elijah asked. "That's not exactly common either."

He had a point. I studied the tape more carefully. "Look, it's dated the same year as one of the calendars I found with the wishing stones," I said, thinking back. "That has to mean they belonged to the same person, right?"

Elijah's face lit up. "We can try to search for people named 'Gem' who lived in town in the 1990s."

We used Elijah's phone to google it, but what little info we could find from that time wasn't helpful.

"Maybe she didn't even live in town," I pointed out.

"I'll stop at the library on my way home and look up old town records. That might tell us if Gem lived here back then."

I looked at my watch. "I should get home. But I'll take this mixtape and listen to it. My dad has an old tape player in our garage. I can see if it still works."

Elijah nodded. "I guess if you don't want your future wishes getting messed up, any research we do might help."

"Wait, what future wishes? The wishes I've made have done enough. Really, I should throw those stones away!"

Elijah's eyes widened. "What are you talking about? You can't get rid of them! Think of all the good you could do with them."

"But I haven't done a lot of good, not really. Yes, Austin's better, but only sort of. Everything else is even more complicated than it was before." I shook my head. "No more wishes. Not until we figure out how this all works."

Maybe not ever.

Chapter 16

When I got home from the shop, I made a quick stop in the garage. After a little searching, I dug up my dad's old tape player from the pile of ancient stuff that my parents hadn't let me throw out when I'd life-hacked the garage last summer. The cassette player was dusty and the clear plastic part was a little cracked, but when I popped the tape in and pressed play, music flared to life on the headphones.

I tucked the tape player in my sweatshirt pocket and headed into the house, but I noticed something strange in the backyard. There were several small mounds of dirt on the edges of the grass. When I went to investigate, I almost fell into a hole that looked like an entrance to a tunnel. Definitely not the usual chipmunk holes we got in our yard. This was bigger, much bigger. An Austin-sized hole, I realized.

"Austin?" I called, peering inside. There was no squeak in response. That probably meant he was in his room sleeping again. He'd been doing that a lot actually—sleeping more and more during the day and then spending all night working on his weird projects.

I let out a deep sigh and turned to go into the house, but then I noticed something inside the tunnel. I knelt down, reached into the dirt, and pulled out a handful of crackers. When I leaned in to get a better look, I realized there was lots more food tucked inside the tunnel: grapes and Cheerios and a bunch of Austin's other favorite foods.

Oh god. He was storing up food for the winter. Austin was going to try to hibernate here!

I got to my feet and hurried toward the house. I had to figure out how to fix this. I just had to.

As I closed the door behind me, I heard shouting. My parents were arguing again. Only why were they both home? Shouldn't Mom still be at work?

"I thought if we could get him healthy, everything would be all right," Dad was saying. "But it never ends!"

Oh no. Had Austin hurt himself while digging all those tunnels?

But then Mom chimed in. "We'll get through this. We always do. I'll find another job—"

"I can't believe they'd fire you because you had to take time off to be with your sick child. It's immoral, and probably illegal!"

My mouth fell open. "Mom, you got fired?" I cried, charging into the kitchen.

My parents froze, and it was obvious in their horrified expressions that they hadn't been planning to tell me the truth.

"We're going to be fine," Mom said. "It's a minor setback, that's all."

But I barely heard her. Because Dad was right. It never ended! Even with luck on our side, things kept getting worse!

"Lexi," Dad began, but I didn't want to hear my parents reassuring me that everything was going to be okay. So I turned and ran up the stairs. As I passed Austin's room, I heard him squeaking away to himself, but I covered my ears until I was in the safety of my room. Then I slammed the door shut and threw myself down on my bed.

After all that time I'd spent trying to keep the universe happy, all it did was keep chewing us up and spitting us out. No matter what I did, it was wrong, wrong, wrong!

I lay there for a little while, glaring up at the ceiling as if this whole mess were somehow its fault. Downstairs, my parents' voices grew louder, arguing again.

I noticed something digging into my hip, and I realized it was the cassette player in my pocket. I pulled it out and slipped on the headphones. As the music sounded again, loud and angry, it perfectly matched my mood.

Maybe those grunge people knew what they were doing, because after a few minutes, my heart stopped drumming in my chest and I started to breathe again. It felt as though someone understood. That someone else was as fed up as I was.

After a few songs, a slower one came on that made me sit straight up. It was the song I'd sang during my audition—the Sally one! When I glanced at the list of songs handwritten inside the cassette tape case, I saw it was by a band called Oasis. Suddenly, I remembered a T-shirt with that same name on it in the box of things I'd been going through when I found the wishing stones. This couldn't be a coincidence. It proved that whoever "Gem" was, the stones had once belonged to her.

I fast-forwarded through the song, since the last thing I wanted to do was relive that horrible audition. Then I lay back when a softer, quieter song came on.

Eventually, I dozed off. When I woke up, the headphones were still on my head but there was no sound coming out of them. The tape must have ended. I sat up and yawned, and my jaw let out two deafening cracks.

That's when I realized that I'd made a decision. It must have come while I was asleep.

Even though I said I wasn't going to, even though I knew it was probably a bad idea, I didn't have a choice. I was going to make another wish.

I dug out the wishing stones and pulled out the Family stone. I almost laughed when I saw that little word etched into it, as if it had been waiting for this. As if it had known that I would need it one day.

I mulled over the wording of my wish for a while, not wanting to mess anything up this time. Finally, I settled on a wish that I couldn't imagine backfiring.

Then I closed my eyes, wrapped my fingers around the stone, and whispered, "I wish my family could be happy."

❉   ❉   ❉

When Mom came to get me for dinner, she was all smiles. "Guess who's downstairs." I couldn't tell if my wish had worked, or if she was only pretending that everything was okay.

"Who?" I asked, suddenly nervous.

"Come and see!" she chirped.

When I got to the dining room, there was a take-out feast of Thai food spread out on the table. I was surprised to see Aunt Glinda sitting in Dad's usual chair, a plate of noodles in front of her.

"Hey, Aunt Glinda! What are you doing here?" I asked.

"Your aunt is joining us for dinner, that's all," Mom said. She gave me a meaningful look across the table, and I wondered if this was all thanks to the conversation we'd had in the car the other day.

"She brought chocolate chip cookies!" Dad chimed in. He was all smiles too, which had to be fake since he was definitely not a fan of my aunt's cooking.

"They're store-bought," Aunt Glinda admitted.

"That's okay!" Mom said. "We really don't mind!"

I could see Dad trying not to laugh. There was something about the air in the room. It felt different. Less heavy than usual. I felt myself relaxing a little as I grabbed a plate.

"Where's Austin?" Mom asked. "Austin! Dinner!"

I held my breath, hoping that my brother would be back to his old self. Then I'd know for sure that my wish was working. But a minute later, Austin barreled in from the family room inside a giant clear exercise ball. And I mean *in* it. He'd somehow taken Mom's old ball, cut a hole in the side, made a bunch of air holes, climbed inside, and closed up the flap. It was like a giant hamster ball. The whole contraption was ridiculous, and it barely even worked since the ball was mostly deflated. But Austin had never looked happier.

Weirder still, everyone else laughed when they saw him.

"Oh, Austin," Mom said. "Your imagination just doesn't quit!"

Dad was laughing too, a big, real belly laugh. The huge fight I'd heard earlier seemed to be long forgotten. Okay, my wish *had* to be working. My family did seem happy.

"Mom?" I asked. "Are you still fired?"

Her smile faded slightly. "I'm afraid so, honey. But don't worry. I have a few leads on some jobs, and I even have a phone interview set up for tomorrow."

"What if you don't get any of them?" I asked.

She patted me on the shoulder. "Let me do the worrying, okay? Everything is going to be fine. Trust me."

"Okay, let's dig in!" Dad said.

And we did. Even Austin came out of his ball for a bit to curl up in his chair and eat noodles with his hands instead of with utensils. Everyone was eating and chatting and laughing. It was like a scene out of a movie.

Even though things felt far from perfect, they actually felt okay. At least for now.

After dinner, I helped load up the dishwasher. As I worked, I started humming one of the tunes I'd heard on the mixtape.

"Oh," Aunt Glinda said. "I haven't heard that song in forever!"

I froze, mortified that I'd been caught singing in my terrible voice again. But then my aunt started singing the next part of the song, and I couldn't help joining in. For a minute, we actually sounded pretty good. Then I messed up the next verse, and she laughed. "We should take our show on the road."

My smile faded as I remembered my audition again. No way. I was never ever, ever going to get up onstage again.

After we finished the dishes, Dad started handing out cookies to everyone in exchange for knock-knock jokes.

"Oh boy," Mom said. "I bet he'll be telling those over and over for the next week."

We all laughed when Dad put his hands up, a cookie in each one, and said, "Guilty."

Then it was time for Aunt Glinda to head home. "Thanks for having me over," she said, giving my mom a quick hug. "You're right. It *is* nice to get out of the house once in a while."

"You're always welcome here," Mom said, hugging her back. "You know that."

I could tell from the mistiness in my aunt's eyes that she hadn't known that. Suddenly, I felt bad about how much I'd been judging her. No matter how overly emotional she was, she was still family. That's why my wish had brought her to us tonight.

Chapter 17

"Lex, you made it!" Cassa cried when I ran into her before first period the next day.

"Huh?" Why was she suddenly so happy to see me? She hadn't even been at the footbridge that morning. I figured it was because she was ignoring me.

Cassa laughed. "The dance club. You made it to the next round."

"Yeah, very funny." I hadn't even bothered checking the list when I'd gotten to school since I'd known I wouldn't be on it.

"Really! Come on. Let's go look if you don't believe me."

I didn't believe her, so I hurried to Miss Flores's office and glanced at the list of kids who'd made it to the final round of dance auditions. There it was, Alexandra Block.

"But I was a disaster!" I said.

"Obviously not," Cassa replied.

I couldn't believe it. Did that mean my dancing had actually been good, despite my horribly embarrassing singing?

"You'll get into the club for sure!" Cassa said. Even though things had been so off between us lately, I could tell that she was happy for me. Maybe our friendship wasn't as doomed as I'd thought.

It only took a second for my excitement to fade as I remembered belting out the Sally song. I couldn't audition, not again. Not until I figured out how to undo the singing curse I'd accidentally put on myself. There was no way I was going to put myself through that humiliation again.

"Whoa," Cassa said. "Marina's on the list too."

That wasn't a surprise, of course, but it still kind of stung to think she might make the team when I wouldn't.

"You didn't tell me she was there," Cassa went on.

"Was I supposed to?"

"Um, yeah! It would be nice to know that someone's actually seen her alive!" Thankfully the school administration had pulled down the "missing" flyers, calling them a prank, but Cassa was still convinced that something fishy was going on. "How did Marina seem? Did she talk to you or anything?"

"Why are you so obsessed with Marina?" I couldn't help asking. "You two have only been hanging out for a few months. It's not like she's your best friend or anything!"

"I'm not obsessed!" Cassa said. "I just don't get it. I thought she'd at least apologize for making us fail our social studies project."

"Wait, you *failed*?" With everything else that had been going on, I hadn't had a chance to send Cassa any more of my research.

"My mom was so mad when she found out," Cassa said. "She made me explain the situation to the teacher, and he said he didn't want to get caught up in our 'little drama.'" She rolled her eyes. "He did agree to let us revise what we did and hand it in next week for a better grade. But only if we work together this time."

I shook my head. How on earth was I going to make that happen?

I realized Cassa was shaking her head too. "I don't know," she said, half to herself. "Maybe it's a sign."

"A sign of what?" She was starting to sound like me.

"It's just . . . I wanted this year to be different. Maybe this is proof that I made the wrong decision."

"Why do things have to be different? Why can't they be good like they've always been?" I demanded. Then I stopped. "Wait. What decision?"

But at that moment the warning bell rang. "Forget it," Cassa said. "It doesn't matter." She shook her head and hurried away.

❀   ❀   ❀

When I got to first period, Mrs. Connor handed me a detention slip the moment I walked through the door.

"What's this?" I asked in disbelief. "The late bell didn't even ring yet!"

"It came from the main office," she said. "You have an unexcused absence."

"Wh-what?" Suddenly, I realized what she was talking about. I'd missed school to go see Austin in the hospital last week, and even though I'd reminded my parents to send the school a note, they must have forgotten with everything else going on.

When I tried to explain that to Mrs. Connor, she shook her head sadly. "You can go speak to the guidance counselor," she said. "But I'm afraid I can't undo the detention. I'll see you at lunch again today, okay?"

I definitely didn't want to see the counselor—there was no way I could even begin to explain my problems to her—so I stopped arguing and took the slip. My third detention in a week. It felt as though I were some alternate version of myself, a Lexi who got in trouble and was late for things and wasn't perfect at math. I didn't like this new Lexi, but the more I tried to get rid of her, the more determined she seemed to stick around.

❉　❉　❉

When I got to lunch detention later that day, Mrs. Connor announced that we'd be working in pairs again and talking about our feelings. When she asked Felix to partner up with me, I was surprised when he called out, "Can't I work with someone else?"

Mrs. Connor shook her head and moved on to the next person. Great. Now Felix didn't even want to talk to me, and I was supposed to be his best customer!

Even though I was offended, I had no choice but to pull my desk over to his. "Are you still here for selling things on school property?" I couldn't help asking. By my count, he should have been done with detention already.

Felix didn't look up from his desk. "Um, not exactly. It's, um, for something else." I waited for him to go on, but he didn't.

Huh. Whatever it was, he clearly didn't want to talk about it. But that was too bad for him, since that's exactly what we were supposed to talk about.

"Okay, so . . . how were you feeling when you, um, did whatever it was you did to wind up here?" I asked.

Felix shrugged. "Annoyed, I guess. At getting caught."

"And, er, what made you feel that way?"

He took a deep breath. Finally, he leaned forward and said, "Okay, look. I'll tell you the truth because you'll find out from someone else anyway. I'm here because I got into a fight with a kid after school yesterday."

"Why wouldn't you want to tell me that?"

"Because of what the fight was about. He found out that . . ." Felix lowered his voice. "That my clovers are fake."

I blinked. "Fake?"

"Oh, come on, Lexi. Don't look so surprised. You had to know they weren't the real thing."

Not real? The four-leaf clovers *weren't real*?

Felix must have seen the shock on my face because he shook his head and said, "Seriously? Where did you think I found them all?"

"I—I guess I thought you were super lucky."

"I glued them together, okay? Just stuck an extra leaf on there and packaged them up."

I thought of my coin purse, stuffed full of dozens of clovers. All of them glued. All of them fake. I suddenly wanted to throw up. Was this what Felix had meant the other day about "making your own luck"?

Of course I should have known it was all a hoax. He'd even tried to warn me not to waste my money!

Felix was giving me a pitying look. "You don't really believe in all that luck stuff, do you?"

Did I? I'd thought of the clovers as an insurance policy, a way to add another layer of good luck into my life, just in case. And now it turned out it was all a lie. A fake, glued-together lie.

"How could you do that to people?" I demanded. "How could you mess with their lives like that?"

Now it was Felix's turn to look stunned. "I . . . I didn't think anyone would take it so seriously. My family's been having a hard time ever since we had to put my grandmother in a nursing home. I thought maybe I could help out by making some cash on the side." He shook his head. "I never meant to hurt anyone."

"Well, you did!" I cried.

But of course I wasn't really yelling at Felix. I was yelling at myself. Because what he'd done with the four-leaf clovers was low, but what I'd done with the wishing stones was even lower. I doubted Felix's scheme had hurt anyone nearly as much as my wishes had.

Chapter 18

When I left school, Elijah was waiting for me on the front steps. He looked as though he was about to burst with excitement.

"I found something at the library about Gem that might help us figure out where the stones came from," he said.

"Really?" Finally, some good news!

He nodded so fast that his glasses slid down his nose. "There was no record of anyone named Gem living in town in the 1990s, *but* there was a woman named Gemini Matthews who opened up that bead shop in town."

"Beady Buy?" I asked, thinking of the place where Marina had dragged Cassa on the day I'd found the wishing stones. Elijah nodded. "Do you think it could be her?"

"It might be," he said. "And the best part is, she still runs the store. If we go see her right now, we can ask about the tape."

"Elijah, you're a genius! But I need to get home and watch my brother while my mom has a phone interview for a new job."

Elijah's excitement deflated. "This is *your* mystery we're trying to solve, remember?"

"I know, and I'm glad you're helping. But it's going to have to wait, okay?"

I figured Elijah could understand that, but he got a strange look on his face. "I can't believe you're going to blow me off," he said. "I thought we were best friends."

I blinked at him. Huh?

"Now you don't even want to hang out with me?" he went on. "What's up with that?"

He sounded hurt, which made no sense. "Elijah, it's nothing personal. I have to get home, that's all. Besides, I told you. Cassa's my best friend."

"So where is she?" he demanded. "I never see you two together."

"That's none of your business," I snapped.

"Fine," he said, his jaw tightening. "If that's how you feel, maybe we weren't meant to be friend soul mates after all."

Friend soul mates? What on earth was he talking about? This didn't sound like Elijah at all!

Before I could try to reason with him, he was hopping on his skateboard.

"Elijah! I'm sorry!" I called after him, even though I wasn't sure what I was apologizing for. But he was already halfway down the street.

❀   ❀   ❀

As I watched Austin playing in the yard while my mom had her interview, I couldn't stop thinking about Elijah and all the stuff he'd said about Cassa. It didn't matter, I told myself. I didn't need friends anyway. I was fine on my own.

I swallowed the aching feeling in my throat and went back to watching Austin dig around in his tunnels.

"Buddy?" I asked, going over to kneel beside him. "Um, are you okay? You're not . . . you're not miserable like this, are you?"

He gave me a few squeaks and then he smiled. At least he didn't seem unhappy, but that didn't mean he could stay this way.

"Kids!" Mom cried, practically skipping out of the house. "I got it! I got the job."

I jumped to my feet. "Really? That was fast."

"They just had someone quit and are desperate to fill the position. And get this. It has more flexible hours and better pay. That means your dad won't have to go on so many trips anymore. It's like a dream come true!"

This had to be because of my Family wish. Finally, one of the stones was working the way it was supposed to!

"When do you start?" I asked.

"If all goes well, next week," she said. "Austin's been healing so well, he should be able to go back to preschool any day now."

My brother let out a loud squeak, hopped back into his exercise ball, and thundered off toward the other end of the yard.

Mom's smile faded as she watched him. "I've never seen Austin play the same game for this long," she said. "And he's been so nonverbal lately, almost like he's regressing. Maybe I should call the doctor."

The last thing my family needed was another medical bill to worry about.

"He's just being a kid," I said, a little too loudly. "I'm sure he's fine."

Mom nodded, but I could tell she wasn't convinced. Which meant I was running out of time.

Chapter 19

The next day, I finally headed to the cafeteria instead of to lunchtime detention. Between that and the day I'd missed because of Austin being in the hospital, it had been over a week since I'd eaten with Cassa. For the first time, I wondered what she'd done during all those days. Had she sat at our table alone, reading history books?

When I got to our usual table, it was empty. Huh. Maybe Cassa had gone to the library the way I did on the days when she was out sick. I thought about going there to find her, to let her know it was safe to come back to the cafeteria.

Then I heard her laugh echoing nearby.

I turned to see Cassa sitting with a table of kids I barely knew. She was giggling away with Kallie Krueger, as if the two of them had been friends for years. What on earth? How did they even know each other? Kallie had moved to town a couple of years ago, but Cassa and I hadn't really talked to her.

For a second, I wasn't sure what to do. Finally, I managed to catch Cassa's eye, and her laughter died. She said something to the other girls and then she picked up her lunch and headed over to me.

"Lex, I didn't know if you'd be here today," she said, sliding into the seat beside me.

"I figured you might be at the library."

She shrugged. "I thought about going there when you weren't here that first day, but Kallie said I should come sit with her."

"How do you know her?"

"I met her at the knitting club meeting. She grew up in England, so she's been telling me all about it."

I couldn't believe it. It was happening all over again. I'd gotten Marina out of the picture, and now Kallie was swooping in to take her place.

"Oh . . . cool," I managed to say.

"She even knows the town where my dad's been living," Cassa went on excitedly. "She said her mom grew up there. It sounds adorable. I can't wait to go visit."

I sat up. "You're going to visit your dad? When?"

"This summer probably." For some reason, Cassa wouldn't look up from her lunch.

"For the whole summer?" I pressed.

"Or part of it. I don't know yet." She cleared her throat. "I'm still figuring it out."

"What about . . ." But I couldn't finish that sentence. Because "What about me?" sounded so silly and so selfish. Just because we usually spent the summers swimming at the town pool and riding our bikes to the library and making rainbow Popsicles from scratch, clearly that didn't matter to her.

"It's still months away," she said. "It might not even happen." She cleared her throat again and then looked up at me. "We'll always be friends. Nothing's going to change that."

But that wasn't true. Things had already changed between us. And the more I tried to keep them the same, the more out of control they got.

❊　❊　❊

Instead of heading home after school, I went over to Beady Buy to follow the Gem lead that Elijah had told me about.

When I ducked into the bead store, the first person I saw at the counter was Marina. Ugh. Okay, universe. I get it. You don't have to keep rubbing her presence in my face!

"I don't know what to do," I heard her saying to the old lady behind the counter.

"I'm sorry, love," the lady said to her. "It's tough when you have a good thing and then things go south. But hang in there, okay?"

Marina nodded, and she looked sadder than I'd ever seen her. Was this because of everything with Cassa?

At that moment, I accidentally bumped into a shelf of jingling earrings. Marina turned, and her eyes narrowed when she saw me.

"Um, hi," I blurted out.

"Oh, so you *can* see me?" Marina said. "You've only been pretending that I'm invisible, is that it? Just like Cassa won't even be in the same room as me anymore?"

I opened my mouth to say something, but she only glared at me and rushed out of the store.

"Can I help you?" the lady behind the counter called out to me. She had a gold beaded headband in her gray hair that made her look like an elderly princess.

"Yes, hi. Um, are you Gemini?"

She smiled. "Most people call me Mimi, but yes, that's me."

"Did you ever go by Gem?"

She shook her head. "To be honest, I've always been a bit embarrassed by my name. Why do you ask?"

"I'm trying to find someone named Gem. I think she grew up here. She would have been my age about twenty-five years ago."

"I've been in this town all my life and I can't remember anyone with that name. And trust me, I would have remembered."

"Okay, thanks," I said, disappointed. Clearly, this lead was a dead end. If Gemini wasn't Gem, then I had no idea where to look next.

I turned to leave, but Mimi called out, "That girl who was just here. Do you two go to school together?"

"Yeah, she's in my grade."

"Well, would you do me a favor and be extra nice to her? It's tough being at a new school. She and her family move around a lot, and I think she's looking for some roots, you know?"

I tried to imagine what Marina's life was like, changing schools all the time, moving around year after year. It had all sounded so glamorous when Cassa talked about it. But honestly, if I were Marina, I'd probably want some roots too. Maybe I'd be so desperate to make new friends that I might not even notice that I was taking away someone else's best friend.

Okay, maybe I'd been a little hard on Marina, but she'd been trying to take *my* roots away from me. I couldn't let that happen, could I?

So I only shrugged, thanked Mimi for her time, and hurried out of the store.

Chapter 20

When I got home, I was surprised to find Aunt Glinda there waiting for me. My insides lurched.

"Is everything okay? Where's Austin?" I asked.

"He's fine. Everyone's fine," she assured me. "Your mom had to go in to her new office to fill out some paperwork, and your dad took Austin to a follow-up doctor's appointment. They asked me to be here when you got back."

I closed my eyes as my heart slowed to its normal thumping. Would I spend the rest of my life jumping to the worst conclusions? Was this how things were going to be from now on?

"I was thinking of cleaning out the attic this weekend," my aunt said. "Any chance you'd feel like helping me? I can pay you in cookies."

"Sure." I certainly didn't have anything else going on. Cassa hadn't said a word about our usual Saturday-night plans. Honestly, I was kind of hoping she'd forget about them. "Don't worry about the cookies, though. I'll do it for free."

"You're the best, Lexi," my aunt said. "I'm so glad we're getting to spend more time together."

"Me too," I said, and I actually meant it.

"So, what do you want to do now?" my aunt asked.

"I'm supposed start on my homework."

She smiled. "If you want to put that off for a while, I brought over some music," she said. "Stuff I listened to back when I was your age. I found some tapes when I was cleaning out the guest room closet. Considering you and I have similar taste in music, I thought you might enjoy going through them."

"Oh, sure," I said.

She laughed. "But I realized no one has tape players anymore!"

"Actually, I do. Hold on a sec." I went up to my room to grab Dad's old one. Maybe we could hook it up to the stereo and both listen to it somehow.

I brought it back down and my aunt's face lit up. "A Walkman," she said. "I haven't seen one of those in ages!" She took it out of my hands and turned it over carefully, as if she were holding a priceless antique.

Then she let out a little gasp. "Where did you get this?"

"The Walkman? It was Dad's. I found it in the garage."

"No, this." She opened the tape player and took out the cassette inside. It was the mixtape with "For Gem" written on it. "Where did this come from?"

There was an odd tone in her voice, almost an accusing one. "I didn't steal it or anything," I said. "It was at the Antique Barn and Ms. Hinkley said I could take it and . . ." I sucked in a breath. "Wait, do you recognize this tape? Do you know who it belonged to?"

My aunt nodded slowly, her eyes still glued to the cassette.

I almost jumped up with excitement. "So who is she? Who's Gem? Do you know her?"

Aunt Glinda sighed. "Once upon a time, Gem was me."

I could only stare at her for a second. "You?" I finally managed. "But . . . but, how?"

"It was a nickname I had back in middle school. Honestly, no one ever called me that besides my friend Deedee. Glinda was a sparkly good witch, right? Well, Deedee would always tease me about my name being glittery and sparkly, and somehow that turned into her calling me 'Gem.'"

"So this tape was for you?"

"Yes, Deedee made it for me before she moved away. I was looking for it everywhere, but I couldn't find it. I thought it was lost." She looked at me. "This was at the Antique Barn?"

I nodded. "In a box with a bunch of other stuff, calendars and things."

"Ah. I guess I should have gone through them more carefully before I dropped them off."

My brain was spinning. It wasn't possible, was it? "So does that mean . . . the wishing stones I found, were those yours too?"

"Wishing stones?" my aunt repeated. "What wishing stones?"

But they had to be hers, didn't they? It was the only thing that made sense.

I ran over to my backpack and pulled them out of the inner pocket where I'd carefully hidden them away. When I brought them over to show my aunt, she blinked at them in surprise.

"Oh! These things!" She laughed. "I'd forgotten all about them!"

That couldn't be right. If she'd made wishes on them, wouldn't she remember?

"Where did they come from? Did you ever use them?" I asked.

"I must have gotten them when I was about your age. They came from a little gift shop in town, one that doesn't even exist anymore. I don't know what possessed me to waste my allowance on them. Anyway, I made a few wishes, but I don't know that any of them came true."

"Do you remember what you wished for?"

"Hmm." She took the stones out of the pouch and looked at each one for a moment. Then she laughed softly. "The Health stone. Oh yes, I remember now. My pet hamster was sick. Captain Squeak, I told you about him the other day. I was scared he was going to die, so I used that stone to wish that he'd be healthy again."

"Did it work?" I asked.

"I have no idea. A few days later, he ran away and I never saw him again."

Okay. Well, that didn't mean her wish hadn't worked. For all we knew, that hamster was still running around, all these years later, healthy as could be. That had to be why Austin was acting so weird, right? Because my wish had gotten tangled up with my aunt's, and the stone had started to make Austin act like a healthy hamster?

"What about the others?" I asked.

My aunt picked up the Success stone. "Oh, this one I used before the talent show," she said. "I wanted to wow everyone with my singing."

"So what happened?"

"Nothing. I got cold feet before the show and never tried singing in front of people again."

"But why?" Her wish would have made her win for sure.

"Because I got scared that I'd mess up. There were too many things out of my control, you know?"

Of course, I did know. It was the exact reason I'd chickened out of auditioning for the dance club last year.

"Family," my aunt said, looking at the stones again. "I don't remember what I used that one for. Probably something silly like wishing my family were happy." She glanced at me. "And we were happy, I suppose. Before your mom went away to college and both of our parents passed on, things were actually really nice." She sighed. "But I guess life runs its course, whatever you wish for."

It made sense that nothing too bizarre had happened with my Family wish, since my aunt and I had pretty much wished for the same thing.

"And the Friendship stone?" I asked.

"That one is easy. I used it to get Deedee Lewis to become my best friend." Aunt Glinda laughed. "My 'friend soul mate,' in fact. But of course, that only worked for about a month. Then Deedee's mom got a new job and they moved away over the summer. I never saw her again."

"Friend soul mate," I repeated in a whisper. It was exactly what Elijah had said the other day. That couldn't be a coincidence.

Then it hit me. Elijah *Lewis*-Green. Was it possible that Deedee Lewis was Elijah's Mama Dee?

No. It couldn't be. Elijah had nothing to do with my wish. He was a nice guy who'd offered to help me out, that was all.

A guy who always happened to come along at the exact right time when I needed him? Who showed up at Aunt Glinda's house with a picture for Austin when there was no way he could have known I was going to be there? Who had become the very friend I needed after everything fell apart with Cassa?

I closed my eyes, suddenly feeling dizzy.

"Lexi? Are you okay?" Aunt Glinda asked.

"Could you give me a ride to Elijah's house? I really need to talk to him."

Chapter 21

When I got to Elijah's, I tried knocking on the front
door, but no one answered. After hesitating for a minute,
I went around the side of the house and knocked on the
shed door. I could hear faint music coming from inside.

I knocked again, louder this time, and the door
swung open.

"Oh, hey!" Elijah said. His shirt was smeared with
paint, and even his glasses had a dab of orange on them.
He looked happy to see me. Too happy considering how
mad he'd been the last time we talked. It had to be part
of whatever the wish had done to him.

"Can I talk to you?" I asked.

"Sure! Come in." He ushered me inside where a large canvas was splattered with all colors of the rainbow.

He looked at me expectantly, but I couldn't make myself tell him about my suspicions. "I found Gemini," I said instead. "Thanks for tracking her down, by the way."

"Did it help? Was she Gem?"

"Um, no. It turns out my aunt was Gem."

His eyelashes fluttered in surprise. "No way! Your aunt Glinda?"

"Yeah. She was the one who used to own the wishing stones." I told him about her wishes, going through them one by one. He nodded, as if it all added up. Finally, I said, "And she used the Friendship one to get a girl named Deedee Lewis to become her best friend."

Elijah took a step back. "Deedee Lewis? That's my mom's name. Or it was, before she got married and hyphenated it."

"Did she live here when she was younger?"

"Yeah, but not for very long. When we moved to town when I was a kid, Mama Dee said she'd always wanted to come back."

So it was true. To think, my aunt's former best friend was living a block away and she had no idea. It sounded impossible, but considering how Aunt Glinda only went to work and came home and never talked to anyone, it actually wasn't that far-fetched.

But if that part was true, then that meant the rest of it was true too. I took in a long, shaky breath and forced myself to say, "I think that's why you showed up in my life when you did, because of that wish."

Elijah pushed his glasses up his nose. "What are you talking about?"

"How did you know I was going to be at my aunt's house that day when you came over to give me the Batman drawing for Austin?"

He thought for a second. "I don't know. I guess I just figured it out."

"But how? You barely knew me, and you didn't know my aunt lived there. I didn't even know I was going to be there until a few hours before."

"I knew I had to bring you that drawing, that's all. Honestly, I drew your brother without even realizing it. It wasn't until I saw you that I knew it was for him."

"Wait, so your mom didn't tell you that Austin was in the hospital?"

Elijah shook his head. "Nah, she's not supposed to talk about stuff like that. I just knew somehow."

"Because of the wishing stones," I said. "They sent you there after I made that wish about Cassa and Marina. My aunt wished for your mom to be her best friend, and somehow that got all twisted up so that the wish sent you to me instead. That's why you've been so nice to me. That's why you didn't care that I'm such a weirdo, because of the wish."

"What are you saying? That we were never really friends?"

"Think about what happened last time we hung out. You got so mad that I wasn't spending enough time with you, remember?"

"Well, yeah, because you were blowing me off."

"No, I was busy. And you acted like we had to spend every second together!"

"Not every second. But if we *are* supposed to be best friends—" He stopped, and I could practically see the wheels turning in his head. "But we're not best friends, are we?" he said slowly. "I mean, why would we be? We barely know each other."

A wave of disappointment crashed through me. So it was true. Our friendship, or whatever it was, had all been fake from the start. Elijah was so confident and relaxed and fun. How could I have ever thought he'd actually want to hang out with me?

"I . . . I have to go," I said.

"Wait," Elijah said. "What about—"

But I was already running out the door.

* * *

When I got home, I tore around my room, trying to find something to organize, but every inch of it had already been life-hacked. There was nothing left to do. Finally, I plopped down at my computer and desperately searched for videos I hadn't seen yet. Then I watched all of them, one after another after another. How to use Vaseline-soaked cotton balls to start a campfire. How to neatly slice a birthday cake with dental floss. How to soothe a cut using ChapStick. I couldn't stop.

As I watched, my brain kept churning. Why did it bother me so much that Elijah might have been hanging out with me because my wish had made him? We'd only gotten to know each other over the past few days, so why was this such a big deal?

Then I realized, maybe that's how Cassa had felt with Marina. Maybe that's why she was so upset that their brand-new friendship had suddenly ended with no explanation.

I was so restless that it felt as though my insides might burst out of my body. Thankfully, I suddenly remembered something that hadn't been organized yet. I jumped to my feet and ran to the kitchen for supplies. Then I grabbed Dad's keys and hurried outside.

I opened Dad's car and pulled out the junk that had been piling up for weeks—take-out containers and used napkins and crumpled receipts—and dumped them in a trash bag. Like I should have dumped the wishing stones the minute I found them. When the car was trash-free, I grabbed a little foam brush and started dusting all the air vents, trying to brush off thoughts of Cassa leaving for the summer. Then I put some baking soda in a sock and stuck it under Dad's seat to suck up the odors, like I wished I could suck up the image of Austin burrowing into the backyard and hibernating all winter.

Finally, I hopped out of the car and started slathering toothpaste all over the car's headlights. I scrubbed and scrubbed, trying to scour away the look on Elijah's face when he said we weren't really friends, but the headlights still didn't look clean.

"Lexi," I heard Dad call from the doorway. "What are you doing out here? It's almost dark."

I was too wrapped up in what I was doing to answer him. I was afraid what might happen if I stopped moving.

"Lex. Lex!" Dad said, coming over to me. "Lexi, stop. Please, put down the toothpaste!" He managed to wrench it out of my hand, and only then did I realize I'd somehow squirted out the entire tube. It was all over me and the car and the driveway.

"What on earth are you doing?" he asked.

But I still couldn't answer him. Instead, I burst into tears.

Dad stood stunned for a second. Then he pulled me into a hug, holding me so tightly that it felt as though he were squeezing all the tears out. Until finally, there were none left.

"You're okay," Dad said into my hair. "Everything's going to be okay."

"You don't know that," I said, pulling away. "How can you know that?"

"Because it has to be," he said, and he sounded so sure. "I know things have been rough lately, but they'll get better. I promise you, they will."

Chapter 22

On Saturday morning, I asked Dad to bring me over to Aunt Glinda's house so that I could help her clean out her attic. The previous day had gone by in a fog, and I was hoping that decluttering something would help pull me out of it.

"Wow, you and your aunt have been spending a lot of time together lately," Dad said. "That's great. I know she loves the company."

I nodded but didn't say anything. Because the truth was, I could use the company too. Unlike with Elijah, at least I knew that my aunt wasn't only spending time with me because some wishing stone told her to.

"How are you feeling?" Dad asked, giving me a long look. "You were in pretty rough shape the other night. Any better now?"

"Yeah, I guess. Sorry again about your car."

He laughed. "Are you kidding? It hasn't been this clean in years. And now it has minty-fresh breath."

I couldn't help letting out a soft laugh. Of course my dad would take my total meltdown and make a joke out of it.

When I got to Aunt Glinda's, she was sitting at her kitchen window again, staring out at the yard, looking ready to cry. For once, my first instinct wasn't to run.

"Are you okay?" I asked, going over to her.

"Oh, yes, fine," she said. I recognized that "fine." It was the one I chanted to everyone, including myself, when everything felt wrong.

"No, really," I said.

She smiled. "I guess thinking about Deedee Lewis the other day brought up all sorts of things. I was always a bit of a loner, you know? Never had a lot of friends. After Deedee moved away, I kind of drifted along by myself. I'm not sure I ever stopped drifting."

"What if I told you that I know where Deedee is?" Maybe I couldn't fix things with Elijah, but at least I could set one thing right.

My aunt wiped her eyes. "What?"

"She lives in your neighborhood! You know Elijah who came over a few days ago? He's her son."

"That's . . . wow, really?"

"So you're not alone. I mean, you have us, you have your family. But if you wanted to, you could have your best friend back too."

I expected her to jump to her feet and dart out the door. But she kept looking at me. "Oh, I don't even know what I'd say to her. I mean, it's been ages. Besides, she probably has her own life and—"

"Those sound like excuses," I said. "I thought you were done making excuses."

It was clear she wasn't convinced. "I'll think about it," she said. Then her face lit up. "Oh, I need to tell you about the stone!"

"What stone?"

"The one I lost," she said. "I completely forgot about it until last night. I was thinking how strange it was that there were only four stones. I mean, what kind of 'magic kit' has four of something? Then I remembered that there used to be five of them."

My mouth fell open. "But what happened to the fifth one?"

"I lost it before I could make a wish on it, probably in the attic. That was my bedroom when I was your age." She shrugged. "Good thing we're cleaning up there today. We might find it."

I could barely breathe. An unused wishing stone. One that wouldn't backfire. One that might actually make everything all right again. Finally, my luck was changing.

✳ ✳ ✳

We spent all afternoon in the attic. I could tell where my aunt had had her bedroom back when she lived up here. One corner was covered in band posters from the '90s, and there was a huge mirror on the wall with old bumper stickers around the edges. I couldn't imagine sleeping up here, crammed in like Austin in his little hamster nest, but I could tell by the way my aunt glanced around at the posters that she had fond memories of being up here. And if this had been where she'd lived, then the stone had to be here somewhere.

With Aunt Glinda's help, I moved furniture, opened endless boxes, and scanned every inch of the space. My mouth was full of dust and I had cobwebs in my hair, but there was still no fifth stone. Not on any of the bookshelves or in any of the boxes or under any of the bedframes. If it was here, it had to be in some nook or cranny where I'd probably never find it. Thanks a lot, universe.

When I finally admitted defeat, Aunt Glinda said, "For all I know, my old hamster ate the stone before he ran away. Maybe it's not even in the house anymore."

That thought was more depressing than I could handle. "I should go get cleaned up. Dad will be here soon."

"Thank you so much for helping me clear out the attic, Lexi," Aunt Glinda said as we made our way back down the narrow stairs. "It looks great in there now!"

That was one good thing that had come out of my frantic search. I'd helped Aunt Glinda get rid of a lot of junk along the way, a lot more quickly than I normally would have. I hadn't had time for any life hacks or organizing tricks, so I'd simply gotten rid of the clutter and tried to put things into neat piles. It actually felt okay to leave it that way, even though it wasn't my usual brand of organized.

"No problem," I said.

"Maybe you could help me tackle Grandma Jean's room sometime." Aunt Glinda laughed, but it was a strained laugh, as if she were fighting back tears again. "To be honest, I haven't even gone in there since she passed."

She looked so sad that I found myself saying, "I'd love to help."

"What about Monday after school?" she asked.

Monday was the second round of dance auditions, but there was no way I was going to that. I might as well come help my aunt instead. "Sure, I'll be here," I said.

She gave me a thumbs-up and brought out some crispy ginger cookies that she'd made. They even looked sort of edible.

❋　❋　❋

When Dad and I got home, I instantly knew that something was wrong. The house reeked of Lysol, and Mom was on her hands and knees scrubbing the kitchen floor. When I thought about it, I realized Mom hadn't gone on one of her de-germing crusades since the day after Austin's surgery.

"What's going on?" I asked. "Where's Austin?"

"He's upstairs napping," Mom said. "I figured I'd tidy up a little in here." Her voice was light, but it was obvious that something had happened.

"How was the doctor's appointment yesterday?" I asked, glancing over at Dad.

He cleared his throat. "Physically, Austin is making great progress. But emotionally, well . . ."

"The doctor is afraid all this stress has been too much for Austin to handle," Mom said. "That's why he's gotten so consumed with his little games."

"What did the doctor say we should do?" I asked. Would he try to put Austin on medication or get him into therapy? Did they even have therapists who dealt with kids who acted like animals?

"He thinks with all of Austin's recent, um, behavioral issues, we might need to take him out of preschool for now," Dad said.

"What?" I cried. "But he loves it there. And if he's not in school, who's going to watch him when Mom's at her new job?"

Mom adjusted her yellow rubber gloves. "I'm going to ask the company to put my application on hold, and I'll reapply for the job in the future."

But that wasn't right. None of this was! What if Austin thought he was a hamster forever? Yes, he was technically healthy, but he wasn't the regular kid he'd always wanted to be. At least with his medical stuff, the doctors could do something to help him. How could they cure a wish?

"Wh-what if Austin doesn't go back to normal?" I asked softly. "Will he be able to go to kindergarten next year?"

Mom gave me a sad smile. "We can't think like that, Lexi. We have to trust that things will work out all right." Then she went back to scrubbing the floor.

Chapter 23

The rest of the weekend went by in a blur of worry. By the time Monday morning rolled around, I was glad to go to school just to have something to distract me from the swirl of stress in my brain.

It didn't even occur to me until I got to lunch that I'd never heard from Cassa about our usual Saturday-night plans. And, even weirder, I'd completely forgotten to stop at the footbridge to wait for her that morning! I wasn't sure what that said about me, or about the current state of our friendship.

Cassa wasn't at our lunch table. When I glanced over to Kallie's table, she wasn't there either. Kallie saw me looking at her and came over.

"Hiya," she said. "You're Lexi, right?" Her accent was so perfectly British that I wasn't surprised Cassa had instantly befriended her.

"Yup, that's me."

"Could you give this to Cassa when she arrives?" she asked, holding out a book. It was a guide to English ruins. "I figure when she moves there, she'll have plenty of time to visit them all."

I was sure I'd misheard her. It had to be the accent. "She's not moving there. She's just thinking of going to visit her dad."

Kallie frowned. "Oh . . . I thought she said she was moving after the new year. She was going to go this summer, but it fell through. I was pretty sure she . . ." She cleared her throat. "Never mind. Maybe I was mistaken." Then she hurried away.

I was frozen for what felt like an hour, trying to process what Kallie had told me. Because suddenly I remembered what Cassa had said about wanting things to be different this year to prove that she'd made the right decision. Was that what she'd meant? Had she been planning to move to England and she hadn't told me?

My eyes must have been about to bug out of my head, because when Cassa finally sat down at the table, it only took her a second to notice that something was wrong.

"Sorry, I had to run to my locker for something. What's going on? Why are you looking at me like that?" She glanced at the book that I still had clutched in my hand. "Where'd you get that?"

"From Kallie," I said through my teeth. "She said you'd need it for when you move to England."

Cassa's face instantly paled. "Oh, Lexi. I . . . I wanted to tell you, but I didn't know how."

I couldn't believe it. How could that be true? "She said you were going to go this past summer but you changed your mind?"

Cassa nodded slowly. "I thought about it. My dad invited me a few months ago. He wanted me to come for the whole school year, but I couldn't just leave you."

"But you can leave me now?"

"No! I mean, I don't want to leave anybody. At least now I know you'll be okay if I go. Now that Austin is better and you don't need me to be there for you all the time."

"What are you talking about? What does this have to do with Austin?"

Cassa slumped in her chair. "The truth is, I've been talking to my dad for a while now. We've gotten a lot closer, and when he told me he was moving to England and he wanted me to come with him, it sounded perfect. I'd finally get to live with him for a while and visit all the cool places I keep reading about and do something different for a change. But then I was scared that if I left, you'd fall apart. You're so used to doing everything the same way all the time. Everything that's different is automatically bad luck. I was afraid that if something happened after I left, you'd think it was my fault!"

"What? Of course it wouldn't be your fault."

"Come on, Lex. What if I moved tomorrow, and the day after that, Austin was in the hospital again? Wouldn't you think you had to get me to move back or he wouldn't get better?"

I wanted to deny it, because when she said it like that, it sounded crazy. But the truth was, that was exactly the kind of thing I would do. I wouldn't think of it as Cassa's fault, but the result would have been the same.

"That's why I decided to stay," she said.

"And that's why you've been acting so weird the past few months," I said. Not just weird. Miserable.

She nodded. "When I met Marina, I thought things would be okay. She'd traveled to all these cool places and done all these awesome things. I thought maybe she and I could go on some adventures together, stuff you'd be too scared to do with me, you know? But then Marina ditched me for no reason, and—"

"That had nothing to do with you," I jumped in.

"It doesn't matter," Cassa said. "I was upset about it at first, but then I realized it wasn't really about Marina ditching me. It was that I'd had a chance to change my life and I hadn't taken it."

"Because of me," I said.

"Not just because of you. I was scared too."

But it *was* my fault. She might not have admitted it, but that's why things had been so strained between us. Cassa had finally found a way to make her life exciting, to do all the things she'd been dreaming about for years, and to get to know her dad again in the process. But she'd given it up for me. And what had I done? I'd made things even worse for her with my stupid wish. I claimed to be her best friend, but what kind of a friend did that? Besides, if I was really her best friend, she would have been able to talk to me about all this stuff instead of hiding it.

"But you've decided to go," I said. "You're leaving in January, and you're not coming back?"

"Actually, I'd leave in December so Dad and I could spend some of Hanukkah together," Cassa said. "We haven't done that in years."

I nodded slowly, trying to make it sink in. In less than three months, Casa would be off on a big adventure without me.

"I wouldn't move there forever," she added. "Probably just for the rest of the school year. And I'd be back this summer. You'd be okay without me, wouldn't you? Now that Austin's feeling better and you're finally making new friends and stuff."

I swallowed. She meant Elijah, but I didn't want to think about him.

As much as I wanted to beg Cassa to change her mind and not go, I knew I couldn't do that. Because as terrified as I was of things changing, I was even more scared of them staying the same. If letting Cassa go meant that I might get my old best friend back, then I had to do it.

"Maybe I could come visit?" I said, trying not to panic at the idea of hurtling through thin air in a metal box with dozens of strangers crammed in next to me. Not to mention finding my way around in a totally different country where people were convinced they *weren't* driving on the wrong side of the road. But if the alternative was spending months and months without seeing my best friend, then it didn't sound that awful.

Cassa let out a surprised laugh. "What? But you hate traveling! It's too unpredictable."

She was right. But that didn't mean she had to be. "Maybe I could change," I told her. "Maybe it's time."

Chapter 24

After school, I hurried past the auditorium, where kids were getting ready for the final round of dance club auditions, telling myself that it was stupid to feel bummed. Even if I could have auditioned without singing at the top of my lungs, I probably wouldn't have gotten in anyway.

I was so busy fleeing the building that I almost crashed into Mrs. Connor in the hallway.

"Slow down, Lexi!" she cried.

I froze, realizing I'd been running—actually *running*—in school! What was wrong with me?

"Please don't send me to detention again," I begged, my voice cracking. I couldn't spend any more lunch periods away from Cassa, not when she'd be gone in a few months. "I won't break the rules again. I promise. I'll do everything perfectly from now on."

"Whoa," Mrs. Connor said. "Relax, Lexi." She glanced around the empty hallway. "I think we can let it slide just this once."

I nodded gratefully, but there were still tears stinging at the back of my throat.

"Is everything all right?" Mrs. Connor asked.

"I just . . . I don't want you to think I'm the kind of person who gets in trouble all the time or gets bad grades. I've never messed up anything before this year, and now I can't seem to stop messing everything up!"

To my surprise, Mrs. Connor smiled. "You know that I almost quit teaching after my first year? Everything I tried kept going wrong. I started to worry that I should have done something else, something safer."

"But you're everyone's favorite teacher!" I cried. Even after those bad grades at the very beginning of the year, I still loved being in Mrs. Connor's class. Math was starting to make sense to me in a way it never had before.

Her smile widened. "Well, I appreciate that. But I wouldn't have gotten very far if I hadn't let myself fail miserably."

"You failed?" I asked in disbelief.

"Oh, yes. That first year, I failed over and over again. I was so determined to do everything right that I got it all wrong. Finally, I stopped trying to be perfect and I started looking for ways to be better."

My watch beeped, telling me I should already be at Aunt Glinda's house.

"Sorry, I really have to go," I said.

"No problem," Mrs. Connor said. "I'll see you tomorrow."

I started off again, but this time at a walk instead of a run. Aunt Glinda certainly wouldn't care if I was a few minutes late. Maybe I shouldn't either.

* * *

When Aunt Glinda opened the door for me, she looked actually glad to see me, not the fake kind of glad that she seemed to put on for everyone else.

"Ready to get your hands dirty again?" she asked.

"Yup," I said. But I wasn't sure she was. When we got to Grandma Jean's bedroom door, Aunt Glinda didn't reach out to open it. Finally, I stepped forward and turned the knob.

I'd expected the room to be a mess, but it wasn't, not exactly. It reminded me of the Antique Barn with its crowded walls and jam-packed shelves, cluttered yet organized. I knew that Grandma Jean had collected elephant figurines, but I had no idea how many of them she'd had.

"Whoa," I said. "There must be hundreds of these." I lightly ran my finger over one of the elephants, and it came away with a coating of dust.

"Three hundred and sixty-five," Aunt Glinda said from the doorway. "One for every day of the year."

"Why so many?"

"Because she thought they brought good luck, and she wanted to make sure she had a little bit of it every day."

Even though it was warm in the room, I shivered. "I wish I had more memories of her," I said softly.

Aunt Glinda laughed. "I have plenty I can share. If you want."

"Sure." I looked around the room. "So what are you planning to do with this place?"

"I used to like sewing," Aunt Glinda said. "I haven't done it in years, but maybe it's time to get back into it. I was thinking I could turn this room into a sewing studio." She sighed. "But what do we do with all these elephants? We can't keep them all."

"I can talk to Cassa's mom," I said. "I bet she'll know."

"It seems awful to get rid of them when your grandmother loved them so much."

"But there's a magic to old things," I said, remembering what Cassa was always saying. "They find their way to people who need them."

Aunt Glinda gave me a tiny smile. "That's a nice way to think about it. And you're right, it's better to give them away than to keep them locked up in here."

Still, she didn't move from the doorway. So I grabbed a duster and some plastic storage bins and started carefully taking the elephants off the shelves, wiping them off, and wrapping them in tissue paper. As I worked, my muscles relaxed. This was like being at the Barn and putting things in order, of making sense out of chaos.

"Do you know how Grandma started her collection?" I asked after a few minutes.

Aunt Glinda smiled. "That's actually a funny story." She took a tiny step into the room, and then another, and then she picked up a small blue elephant from the very top shelf. "This is Leonard," she said. "And Grandma found him on her doorstep." Then she launched into a story about how Grandma kept trying to find the owner but never did. Eventually she accepted that he was hers and that she'd need to find him some friends. "After that, she swore that her luck improved. So she kept collecting and collecting them until she had one for every single day of the year. She said that way Leonard had friends all year round."

"What about on leap years?" I asked.

Aunt Glinda laughed. "You really are so much like her." She picked up a small box on the desk and opened the lid. Inside was a small purple elephant, covered in sparkling glass. "Meet elephant number three hundred and sixty-six. She brought him out once every four years. The rest of the time, she said he was napping in there."

I carefully picked up the elephant, loving the way he sparkled in the sunlight. He felt right in my hand, somehow, as though I was meant to hold him.

Reluctantly, I went to put him back in his case. And that's when I saw it. Inside the small box was a shining gray stone, the size of a chocolate coin.

"Aunt Glinda!" I said with a gasp, holding out the box to her.

She looked inside, her eyebrows arched in surprise. "How did it get here?"

I put the elephant aside and carefully pulled out the stone. It was exactly like the others, except for the writing on the side. This one simply said *Luck*.

❈   ❈   ❈

I ran all the way to the school, hoping it wasn't too late to make it to the end of the audition. When I fell into the auditorium, everyone turned to look at me, and I could tell none of the other kids were happy to see me. No one wanted a belting lunatic hanging around.

Luckily, Miss Flores waved me over and told me I'd be going in the final group again. Then she turned back to the kids on the stage. There were only two groups to go before it was my turn.

I took a deep breath and started warming up just like last time—jogging in place, arm circles, knee bends, and torso twists—since it had seemed to help. But as I went through the movements, the Luck stone grew heavier and heavier in my pocket. I'd found it right before my audition. That had to be a sign. I was supposed to use it to undo my Success wish and nail my audition. Wasn't I?

I stopped mid–knee bend and took the stone out of my pocket. I should make the wish now, before it was too late. I closed my eyes and squeezed the stone tightly in my fingers.

But what about Austin acting like a hamster and Cassa moving away and Elijah being a fake friend? It all needed fixing!

I slipped the stone back into my pocket and bent over to touch my toes. My brain was so heavy that it felt as though it might spill out of my ears. How could I use the last wish on the dance audition when I should use it on Austin? And that still left Cassa and Elijah. Of course, Austin was the most important, but I had no idea how to fix those other things in my life without wishes.

"Lexi?" I heard someone call. I straightened up to find that all the other kids in my group were already up onstage and Miss Flores was waving at me. "Are you joining us?"

Oh no. I hadn't made the wish! As I stumbled toward the stage, barely remembering how to put one foot in front of the other, my thoughts were doing their own frantic dance. How could I audition if my stupid singing curse was still going strong? But I couldn't use the wish on myself. Austin, Cassa, my parents, Elijah, this audition . . . argh! If only I could use one wish to fix everything!

And that's when I realized what I needed to do.

I stopped at the bottom of the steps, pulled the stone out of my pocket, and squeezed it as tightly as I could. Then I whispered, "I wish to undo all my other wishes."

Even though it meant that Austin might get sick again one day and that there was nothing I could do about it. Even if it meant Cassa might stay in England forever and Elijah might never want to actually be friends with me. Even though it meant I had to stop trying to nudge the universe where I wanted it to go and finally trust that things would work out on their own. It was the only way.

When I put the stone back in my pocket, there was no tingly feeling or sudden calm. There was no zing or zap or pop. But somehow, I knew it had worked.

"Lexi?" Miss Flores called again.

"I'm coming!" I said and hurried up to join everyone else. It was only when I was waiting for the music to start that I realized I could have run for the door instead. I didn't have to do this.

But I wanted to. And this time, I wasn't going to chicken out.

So when the music started, and Miss Flores counted down, I tried to forget all the dozens of worries swirling around in my head. All the stuff that could go wrong. Instead, I focused on the one thing I could control: letting myself have fun. After a few twirls, I actually did. I spun and kicked and step-ball-changed.

When it was done, I felt so much lighter. I felt free.

"Thanks, everyone!" Miss Flores called. "I'll post the list tomorrow."

Afterward Miss Flores came up to me. "Great job up there, Lexi," she said. "It was nice to see you enjoying yourself."

I smiled. Because she was right. For a few minutes, at least, I'd just let things be.

Chapter 25

When I got home, Austin was curled up on the couch in front of the TV. Some cartoons were on, but he didn't seem to be watching. He was tearing a piece of construction paper into strips.

"How are you doing, buddy?" I asked, suddenly afraid that I'd been wrong about my wish working.

Then he blinked and glanced up at me. Instead of squeaking or twitching his nose, he smiled. "Okay," he said. Then he grabbed a comic book off the table and asked, "Can you read to Batman with me?"

"Sure," I said, settling on the couch next to him.

He burrowed into my shoulder and mumbled, "LoveyouLexi."

That's how I knew he was really okay.

❊　❊　❊

When Mom and I pulled up in front of Elijah's house after dinner, I sat in the car for a minute, afraid to get out.

"Honey?" Mom asked. "Do you want me to stick around while you go talk to him?" I hadn't told her the details, of course, but I'd explained that Elijah and I had kind of had a fight and that I needed to see if things were okay between us.

"Um, yeah," I said. "That would be nice."

She smiled. "How about I go over to Aunt Glinda's and you meet me there when you're done, okay?"

"I don't think she's home," I said. "The lights were off when we drove by."

Mom laughed. "Of course she's home. She's *always* home. And if not, I have a key." She patted my knee. "Okay, off you go."

I thanked her and got out of the car. I heard music coming from the backyard, so instead of going to the front of the house, I went around and knocked on the shed door. After a long minute, it swung open.

At the sight of me, Elijah flashed an uncertain smile. "Oh, hey," he said. "You're Lexi, right? What are you doing here?"

Something inside me sank. "Um, I wanted to see, um . . ." But it was obvious he didn't remember me, not really. And why would he? If I undid the wish, then he only thought of me as some girl in his class way back when he still went to school. Not someone he was actually kind of friends with now. Someone he'd helped more than he'd ever know.

I blinked back tears. "Sorry, I should go."

I turned to leave, but Elijah called out, "Wait!" When I glanced back, I saw he was holding a couple of the cards we'd made for the kids at the hospital. "These are signed by both of us. Did we work on them together or something?" He laughed and rubbed at a smudge of blue paint on his hand. "It's weird. For some reason, I don't remember."

The tight feeling in my chest eased a little. Maybe the wish hadn't undone everything.

"It was your idea. I just helped."

"These are pretty good. Maybe we can make some more sometime."

"Sure! That would be fun!" I said. Maybe I sounded a little too eager, but I didn't care.

"Good." He flashed me a big grin. "Then my parents can finally stop bugging me about making some friends."

I coughed in surprise. "I didn't know you cared about that kind of stuff."

Elijah shrugged. "I mean, I don't let it get to me or anything, but it would be nice to have someone to hang out with, you know?"

I smiled. "Yeah. I do."

Suddenly, a familiar laugh rang out from the house. I turned to see a woman who I assumed was Mama Dee coming out onto the back deck. Right behind her, carrying a plate of cookies, was Aunt Glinda!

"Whoa! What's my aunt doing here?" I asked.

"That lady's your aunt?" Elijah asked. "It's so weird. She showed up at our door today and my mom freaked out and started hugging her and crying. It turns out they were best friends when they were our age but they haven't seen each other since. Isn't that nuts? All this time they'd been living down the street from each other and they had no idea. It's like magic or something."

I had to laugh. "Maybe," I said. "Or maybe the universe knows what it's doing sometimes."

❋　❋　❋

In the morning, my house was full of chaos the way it normally was. But it was the right kind of chaos. Dad was attempting to get Austin to brush his teeth before preschool while Mom gulped down some coffee before her first day at her new job.

"Remember to head to Aunt Glinda's after school

today," Mom reminded me. "I'll pick you up after work. And thanks for being so flexible about all of this. I know you like things a certain way."

"I did," I said. "I do. But I'm trying to relax a little. Actually, I think Aunt Glinda and I might take a cooking class together."

Mom looked at me in surprise, but I could tell she was excited at the idea of both my aunt and me trying something new. Surprisingly, I was excited too.

"Oh, and we should do another family dinner on Friday," I added.

"Good idea," Dad said, donning his cheesy grin. "We should make it a potluck. You bring the food and I'll bring my appetite."

"It'll be good for us to spend more time together," Mom said. "Hanging out in hospital rooms isn't exactly quality time."

"Can Batman cook something?" Austin asked.

"Um, sure," I said. "What about bat stew?"

Austin giggled. "Bat juice!"

I tickled his belly and couldn't help making sure it didn't seem swollen. But it looked fine. *He* looked fine. And he really was this time. Maybe there was nothing I could do to make sure he stayed that way, but it wasn't up to me. If he got sick again, we'd figure it out, like we always had.

Cassa was waiting for me at the footbridge before school, like normal. But this didn't feel like a normal day. It felt abnormal, different, and exciting.

When we got to the fence at the edge of the school grounds, I was surprised to see Felix leaning against it with a box under his arm.

"Hey, Lexi," he said. "I heard about your dance audition. How about one of these for luck?" He opened the box, revealing a dozen rabbit's feet. "Since you're my best customer, I'll give you one for free."

I should have just kept walking, but I couldn't help asking, "Are they real?"

Felix shrugged. "Does it matter? If you think they'll work, then they probably will."

But I didn't need any more fake luck or secondhand wishes. Last night, I'd hidden the stones in the back of my closet, where I hoped they'd stay forever. Maybe I'd never totally let go of my deal with the universe, but that didn't mean I had to let it control my entire life.

"Thanks," I said. "I think I'm good."

I expected Felix to look disappointed, but instead he nodded approvingly and said, "Good." Then he turned away to flag down another potential customer.

Cassa and I hurried into school and headed over to Miss Flores's door. I was shaking with nerves, but the dance club list wasn't up yet.

"You'll get in for sure," Cassa assured me.

"I hope you're right. And if I don't, I'll try out next year." Now that I'd finally done it, I knew I could do it again.

"Miss Flores better post the list soon or we'll be late to first period," Cassa said. She rolled her eyes. "You don't want Mrs. Connor sending you to detention again."

I laughed. "I'd survive." After all, I already had. "So, um, Cassa," I added softly, afraid to ask the question. "Are you still going to England?"

For a second, I wanted her to tell me that I was insane, that the idea had never even occurred to her. Then I'd know that it was all the wishes' fault and that everything was back to normal again.

But instead she nodded and said, "My dad just sent me info about the school where I'll be going. It's in an old castle! Can you believe it? You'll have to help me figure out what to pack and how to fit everything in my suitcases. You're like a pro at stuff like that."

That was true. And England was still months away. So much could change between now and December. Maybe I should take Elijah's advice and try not to worry about it.

"You better start practicing your sword-fighting skills," I told her. "In case anyone decides to storm the castle."

"Hmm," she said with a smile. "Maybe I should think about becoming a lefty."

At that moment, Marina came around the corner. As usual, my muscles tensed when I saw her. Then Cassa stepped forward and called out, "Hey, stranger! Long time no see! Are we still on for working on our project tonight?"

"Totally," Marina said. "And I'll bring some new beads to show you."

It was still weird to see Cassa so comfortable with someone else, but I was relieved that things between them were back to normal. Especially when Marina turned to me and said, "You were so good at the audition, Lexi. I hope we both get in."

"Thanks," I said. "You were really good too."

When Miss Flores came out with the list, the three of us held hands and shrieked and jumped around when both my and Marina's names were on it. And even though it wasn't at all the way I'd planned it, it was actually kind of perfect.

Acknowledgments

I've always loved stories about wishes. When I woke up in the middle of the night with the phrase "second-hand wishes" in my head, I *had* to turn it into a book—and I had lots of help along the way. Eternal thanks to Patty Bovie, Susan Lynn Meyer, Susan Lubner, Kris Asselin, Heather Kelly, and Erin Dionne for their invaluable feedback and brainstorming help. Thank you to Sarah Allen-Lloyd for patiently answering my questions and to Sarah Chessman for being such an entertaining sounding board. Thank you to my agent, Ammi-Joan Paquette, and my editor, Erin Black, (and the rest of the Scholastic team) for their guidance and expertise. Thanks to my friends and family, particularly to my husband, Ray Brierly, for their patience and encouragement. And finally, thank you to Sara Cole and her family, to whom this book is dedicated and who deserve all the luck in the universe.

About the Author

Anna Staniszewski is the author of several middle-grade novels, including *Once Upon a Cruise*, the Dirt Diary series, and the Switched at First Kiss series. She also wrote the picture books *Power Down*, *Little Robot* and *Dogosaurus Rex*. She lives outside Boston with her family and teaches at Simmons College. When she's not writing, she's out collecting four-leaf clovers and new ideas for life hacks. Visit her online at annastan.com.